JACK HOLBORN

LEON GARFIELD

JACK
HOLBORN

Illustrated by Antony Maitland

LONGMAN YOUNG BOOKS

LONGMAN GROUP LIMITED
London

*Associated companies, branches and representatives
throughout the world*

First published 1964
Fourth impression 1971

ISBN 0 582 15088 4

To Vivien

Printed in Great Britain by
Lowe & Brydone (Printers) Ltd., London

Chapter One

My story must begin when I boarded the *Charming Molly* at Bristol. Before that there's little to tell. My name is Jack, surnamed "Holborn" after the Parish where I was found: for I had neither father nor mother who'd cared enough to leave me a name of their own.

When I was old enough to stand without the aid of my hands, employment was found for them with a stony-fisted cobbler who did nothing but prate about my good fortune in being with him—and curse his own lack of it in having me. When I was old enough to run, I left him. But now, looking back on it, he must have been a virtuous man, who did his charitable duty according to his lights. It was ill-luck that those lights never shone on me.

So I came to Bristol which I judged to be the best place for leaving this hard-hearted, scornful land, where money alone in your purse serves you for honour, justice and pity; and a good heart in your breast serves you for nothing but to break.

It must have been my birthday, for God made me a present of a good black night so's I was able to board the *Charming Molly* as easily as if I'd paid my passage. I pitched on her because she was of a goodish size, smartly rigged, and most conveniently moored. This last was the strongest consideration, travellers in my situation having not much time to make a careful choice. But her figurehead took my fancy, as indeed did her name; and in my wisdom I thought nothing evil could befall a vessel so gallantly called. Where she was bound, I knew not, but hoped it was for savage parts where men went barefoot—my cobbler having left me with a horror of shoes.

I stowed away very comfortably in the hold which was full of barrels and sacks and the perfume of bilge which stank not at all to high heaven (as the saying goes), but kept where it

7

was: for such a stink has no business with the angels. I took a full sack for my pillow and an empty one for my blanket and lay down by the broad mizzen-mast where it met the keel. I meant to stay awake and listen for the crew's returning for news of when we were sailing, but weariness and the vessel's gentle rocking sent me off into a deep sleep from which I awoke to find we were at sea.

I could hear the rigging creak and groan like leather on the last, and now and again came the sharp slap of a sail emptying, then taking a fresh bellyful of wind. Such light as cracked the blackness round the edge of the hatch served only to tell me it was day and I still saw mainly with my hands—which led me very painfully astray . . . We were rolling a good deal, and, though my arms and legs were steady, my stomach began to follow the motion of the waves. This is called sea-sickness and is the most horrible thing in the world, and I lay in the stinking blackness of the hold and prayed to die. I heard the sailors above swearing and shouting and singing; and I cursed them for their good spirits. Loudest of all I heard the voice of the captain striving to rasp the *Charming Molly* along with his windy tongue. As he came and went along the deck, I tried to give that voice a face and form; for I conceived myself to be very soon before him and accounting for my un-lawful presence. By its loudness, tone and vigour, I judged it to come from a man very tall and broad, with fists like boots and a face like a hammer. And for all I know, he might have been ten feet tall, and broad to match: for I never set eyes on that luckless man, even though, sometimes, he was but an arm's length away . . .

All the while the swell of the sea was growing steadily worse, and my sickness with it, till I could do no more than moan for the mercy of a quick end and have done with all my suffering. I heard the captain shouting to make all fast, to haul in the foresail and topsails; and, though I could not see the sky, it must have grown very dark, for the cracks of daylight turned dim—and of a menacing grey. The sailors sang no more, and all there was left between us and silence was the voice of the captain, still shouting. It sounded very bold out there, all by itself, preparing to do battle with the wind and the sea and the sky, for all the world as if the odds was even.

Then the storm—which had lain in wait for us like a wild beast—sprang. They say that a storm at sea is the most terrifying of all disasters. And so it is. If I hadn't been mortally seasick all the while, I'd surely died of fright. Waves turned to rock and thundered on our sides to be let in, while icy water poured down through our upper seams—though which was upper and which was lower in that dark a shipwright would have been hard put to know: for I'll swear there were whole minutes when the *Charming Molly* showed her very keel to heaven!

For a good half of the tempest, my stomach must have thrown up every meal I'd had in my life: for a worse half, I prayed for I don't know what: and for the worst half of all (a storm cares nothing for arithmetic and has as many halves as it chooses) I lay nearly dead of a blow from that thankless sack I'd freed to make me a pillow.

When I came to myself again, I was wet and weak and aching both inside and out. The motion of the ship had subsided and I thought God had grown less angry with the world. I heard steps above me once more, and the sailors singing again.

"There she goes," I heard the captain say, "like a great black tiger in the sky. D'you see her, mister? Long tail and a great paw dripping down into the sea? Murdering beast!" The storm had passed us by.

We continued on our way for an hour or more, during which time I brooded on how best to make myself known to the captain and crew. I'd recovered enough to be hungry and thirsty, and I longed for a sight of the sea and sky. Though I'd little enough to tell, the way of saying it somehow stuck in my throat. With no name but that of a parish, I was a poor addition to any ship's company. So I thought awhile on my vanished mother and wondered if she still lived. This was not a new thought, for many a time at the cobbler's it had come . . .

I used to fancy myself to be of noble blood, snatched for some dark cause, and would look—sonlike—at such elegant ladies who called. Some smiled, some complained, but none looked back motherlike. I thought I had a birthmark once, just above my knee: but it wore away with too much washing—as did the fondest of my dreams. I'd never have abandoned the cobbler if those dreams hadn't abandoned me first.

Still, somewhere I'd had a mother, and that was for certainsure, and wherever in the world she was, I asked her now for her blessing on her forgotten son's enterprise. In another minute, I'd have got my courage and gone up on deck. But I waited for that minute in which I was most surely blessed.

A confused shouting broke out above. Men began running violently across the deck with feet like thunder. A ship had been sighted away to the starboard bow. It seemed she was not above half a mile off and sorely torn by the storm. Her masts were snapped and her rigging carried off, and she was desperately low in the water. She was flying no flag—there was nothing left to fly one from. But good or bad, English or otherwise, it was plain to the sailors above she was not long for this world.

The captain's harsh voice drove the men from pity to action and I felt us tilt sharply as we changed course to starboard. I heard the crack of rope against canvas, which can sometimes be as sharp as musket-fire; and I heard the grunt of sails as they took the wind and we leaped forward joyously on our errand of mercy.

Then our canvas was hauled in and our pace began to drop as we drew close. Presently I could hear the sea slopping the sides of that other vessel in a weary kind of way, as if to say, "I've done with you. Why don't you go to the bottom?" Then I heard grappling ropes flung from ship to ship and made fast. I heard men clambering aboard: fifteen, twenty, even thirty I counted before I began to think there was something amiss.

For none of them spoke a word. Just the thud-thud as their feet landed on the deck, then nothing. Had they been so battered and beaten by the storm that they'd lost the power of thanks, or speech?

A great uneasiness seemed to lie on the ship, and the men of the *Charming Molly* fell as silent as the strangers. It was a very bitter stillness as half a hundred hearts grew cold when they saw what they'd rescued.

"Well, for God's sake!" shouted a single voice—

By way of answer there came a crackling, spiteful roar as between thirty and forty muskets and pistols were discharged into the bellies, brains, hearts and lungs of the rescuers. A great many fell at once, in a clumsy, lumpish manner, tumbling among legs and feet not quick enough to avoid them. Then those who were not hit began running in a despairing kind of way, scudding from side to side, hopping on a turn, till too great a hurry brought its own calamitous reward.

At the beginning, there was a tremendous amount of screaming and shouting and raging to God: then this got less as the need diminished and the murdered sailors understood there was to be nothing for them but dispatch. A few remaining voices cried out women's names with melancholy affection till a loud, full period was put to them, too. Five or six pistol shots concluded the whole, each being followed by its customary grunt of collapse.

A remarkable lad would have gone up in the midst of all this and maybe survived to tell the tale. Maybe. He would have fought with teeth and nails and feet and done some damage before he was stopped.

A less remarkable lad stayed where he was, nine parts out of his mind with terror—and the tenth, wishing himself anywhere else in the world. Every patch of wet his hands slipped into, he conceived to be blood: though it's certain very little dripped through from the deck into the hold. Indeed, the

leaking remains were very quickly posted into the sea—
sometimes two and three at a time, so it was hard to say how
many there had once been.

I think maybe forty, of whom not one, not one! I understood to've survived this last calamity that came out of the
storm. The ship had been taken by pirates.

Chapter Two

WE live in a wicked world wherein pirates and their like are
in the way of nature. Yet most of them, it's said, are poor
enough devils of no great wickedness and not very willing to
ballast their souls with murder. But in and among these lambs
of plunder hunt the terrible wolves—crews so deep in damnation that they cast a black shadow on all sea-going: for they
sail under the Devil's marque and their ships reek with blood.
Such a crew it was that had boarded the *Charming Molly*.

It was near dark when they heaved me out of the hold, and
the sun was setting on the larboard bow, making the sky as
red as the deck. I made no great stir as I came up, no more than
six men turning and staring like I was the last course to a dinner
they'd hoped was done. Their faces were more weary then
wicked, and black with many days' beard. They were very
ragged and filthy in their attire, and looked the more so against
the huge and splendid canvas of the *Charming Molly*: for they
were already in the rigging and on the yards and everywhere
about the ship, with prying hands and eyes discovering if their
prize was sound. The strong sea breezes that blew across the
deck seemed to blow right through my head and make me
drunk, so I was seeing two men for one and eight for four, and
there was nowhere I could turn for mercy or escape.

Then a little man came neatly down from the poop-deck to observe me closer. I took him for the Captain, for he was very brisk in his speech and would have been dapper had there not been something mildewed about him due to his clothes never drying but on his person. He began to question me, quick as musket-fire: and, with each answer, nodded neatly as if flicking it into its proper place . . . answers that told him my state and station, trade and business, my name—he lifted his brows at "Holborn", and dropped them at "Jack".

"Holborn Jack?" (A most notorious rogue of those days.)

"No, sir: Jack Holborn. In honour of the Parish."

He asked my age, too—but there he had me. I said, "Fourteen," and hoped it was an age he was partial to.

The state of my mind he'd no need to ask: it showed plain enough in my face: terror. This seemed to please him, for he opined that gratitude for the sparing of my life would fit me for many a task too humble for those who lived and weren't grateful for it.

For a beginning, then, though the night was almost on us, I was set to cleaning up the maindeck: for, said the little man, there was much danger from the blood; any man might slip on it and break a leg, or worse . . .

I slept that night in the galley, which was the only place I got a welcome. For the cook had thought me worth keeping alive with a lump of pork and a mug of stale water. He'd seen I'd a talent for scrubbing that would have been a shame to lose by an early death.

"Yo're weak and feeble, boy," said he. "Pobjoy'll be mad if you go and die on us."

Somehow, this vile old man, I suppose because he did not offer to murder me for my insolence in being alive, did much to restore my spirits. I even counted him a sort of friend . . .

"Lord save us!" said I. "I'll do no such thing to displease Mister Pobjoy! So cut us another slice of pork!"

"No, dear boy, you'll only womit it up again. And that would be a wicked waste. Pobjoy cannot abide waste."

Rot Mister Pobjoy! I thought, for the little bit of pork that had gone down to my belly was lonely and cried aloud for company. "Mister Pobjoy is a very strict captain."

"That he would be," agreed the cook, scratching his filthy beard, "that he would be—if he was. But bless you dear boy! Pobjoy's the cook! Pobjoy! See?" Then he shook his head: but I think he was flattered to be taken, roundabout, for the captain. So he put me right very kindly and dreamily, as though the arrangement of this dark world was something he'd long brooded on . . .

Though it was right and proper I should respect and look up to Mister Pobjoy, I should understand, here and now, before it was too late, that the Captain was something else entirely. That man and Mister Pobjoy had only mortality in common: and even *that* wasn't certain . . . "*There's* a man for you! Not over big, yet he's a spirit on him that spreads its wings over us like a fallen angel's. There's something wickedly wirtuous about him that makes you touch yore cap when he passes by. All we pore souls sail outside of the law because the winds of ill-luck drive us. But he goes with a wind of his own choosing. And though we all go the same way, his are the only sails that are trimmed."

"I'd never have took him for a better man than you, Mister Pobjoy."

"What? Have you seen him, then?"

"The little man with green breeches and a heavy hand."

"Bless you, dear boy! That's Mister Morris, the sailing master! The Captain's another man altogether!"

Then he fell to asking me what else I knew of the ship. Particularly he asked concerning the hold. ("Barrels, Mister Pobjoy, sir—barrels and barrels!") Was it gin, he wondered, sweet-smelling casks, stacked and secured? Little glow-worms seemed to crawl round his rheumy eyes, and foolishly I tried to please him. "Aye, Mister Pobjoy, there's gin down there—sweet-smelling, all right!"

It seemed I'd slept no more than ten minutes when I was woke with a kick and the good news that the sun was up before me. My day was begun. "God save me!" I muttered.

"What's that! What's that?" shouted Mister Pobjoy. He'd waked to the foulest of tempers and sat with his hair on end and his great hands clutching the edge of the table: a very sour and verminous old man, mad for gin.

"You put a curse on Pobjoy! You said—God rot Pobjoy! His tongue dries up, his skin pricks, his bowels turn over! Go fetch a cask of that gin! It's Pobjoy's desire—now! Or he'll cut yore liver out and give it to the lousy crew for breakfast!"

He grabbed a knife and began to run backwards and forwards across the narrow galley, banging on the pans that got in his way, and stopping only to howl that he was cursed and would perish without his necessary gin.

This, I reflected, was the result of my desire to please. I should have guessed when I saw the glow-worms in his eyes. I'd lit a fire in his head with my tale of gin that only gin would douse. All night the thought of gin must have been festering in his brain—"there's gin aboard"—and one Mister Pobjoy woke the sleeping other and told him. For I'll swear there were two Mister Pobjoys in one. Maybe that's why he never (save once) called himself "me" or "I", but always "he" or "Pobjoy", as though he was but the timid watcher of the deep-down awful Pobjoy—Pobjoy the gin-mad demon who slept till the words were whispered in his invisible ear, "There's gin aboard, Pobjoy . . ."

I bolted under the table. I saw his scarred and scabby feet pounding the boards, and every few seconds his wild face upside down, with his beard in the air, glaring to see where I'd hid.

Then, when I'd given up hope of surviving that morning, a pair of dapperer feet stepped in and a familiar voice bade Mister Pobjoy rest easy in his spirit: that the boy was a poor thing and would do no enormous harm with his liver left in him—and no good with it out. Then I heard Mister Pobjoy stagger heavily against the end of the galley where a roar of copper pans came prosperously down on his head.

I think Mister Morris must have pushed him: but I'm not sure. But I think it's certain that he saved my life—though with his usual brisk unconcern, he left it where it was under the table without ever sparing it a look; saying as he went, "I leave him in your charge, Mister Pobjoy. Do not murder him without first inquiring of me."

Chapter Three

So I was become Pobjoy's boy, Pobjoy's curse, Pobjoy's scab, Pobjoy's meal o'bones, Pobjoy's bag o'skin, Pobjoy's mouse, Pobjoy's rat: and sometimes, when the gin tasted sweet, Pobjoy's apprentice and child. The days stretched out before me as rough and enormous as the great sails of the *Charming Molly* herself: they were indeed canvas days, full of nothing but the wind that drove us on: and in them I discovered that all the dark, hostile Cains that sailed the stolen ship were not so much alike that no man could tell them apart. They had different names, and likes, and changing partialities for one another . . . Also, I found, they were not all as bad as each other: some were for certain worse.

There was a certain Mister Taplow, a red-haired Welshman and walking condensation of hatred for all the meek world. And there were the brothers Fox, Ben and Sam, very loving sons of a dead mother and a hanged father, so their love was in the grave . . . And a gunner called Clarke—and others who daily gave me cause to wish them less than well . . .

Of the Captain there was still nothing to be seen, though his spirit, as Mister Pobjoy foretold, brooded powerfully over the ship. So strong and purposeful blew the wind that he seemed to be master of it, while the men aboard seemed like the wicked children of an invisible wicked father from whom they drew their license to sin. So mine wasn't the only glance that kept straying to the empty companionway, nor mine the only pair of feet that went softly in that part of the ship.

It was on my fourth day aboard (though it seemed more like my fortieth), just past noon—for the sun was between the mainmast and the fore, and I, a bit lower down, was between the mizzen-mast and the main. The mainmast's shadow was too short for me to linger in, and the sun beat down very hot on my back, throwing me into a haze.

I was musing with an idle brush, rocked nearly to sleep by the motion of the ship, when a pair of feet crossed my gaze and halted.

Such shoes the Holborn cobbler would never had let me soil with my life's breath! of the finest Cordova leather that took no crease from the tread. The buckles were of plain gold and bespoke that kind of modesty that is the outward flourish of great pride. My heart began to beat violently, and some

B

forgotten scenes from past life flashed before my mind's eye—
as some say happens when a man drowns. But though I was in
no danger of my life at that moment, I was so supernaturally
frightened that I felt there was mortal danger to my soul.
I looked up, and for the first time saw the Captain of the
Charming Molly.

I got a great shock, for he was not as I'd ever pictured him.
The sun shone full upon him and lent him such radiance and
warmth that I couldn't but exclaim in my heart:

"This is no Captain of murderers! Not this good, kind,
simple-seeming, just man! He is aboard by mistake! He keeps
to his cabin in melancholy at the wickedness of the others."
I got to my feet and would have pulled off my cap, if I'd had
one—just as Mister Pobjoy foretold—for this neatly dressed
gentleman with close-cut grey hair and country complexion
had such an air about him! I couldn't believe he was who he
was, for he stood there so plain and easy, with his legs astride
and his hands behind his back. Maybe his eyes were a little cold
and fish-like, as though they'd looked on more than most men's;
but they seemed to quarrel with his face rather than suit it.

"You must be Jack," he said pleasantly, and, dusting a piece
of deck with his handkerchief, squatted down on the boards.
Dumb with astonishment, I squatted likewise—as he'd signed
me to do—and there we sat, the Captain and me, in the middle
of the deck, like a pair of friends, with the crew going about
their business as if nothing in the world had happened!

"So the fates have made you a pirate! Not a bad life for a
parish boy—if he keeps his wits about him!" He never looked
much at me as he talked, but kept dropping his eyes to the deck
as if not wanting to make me feel ill at ease by too close a
scrutiny.

"A parish boy, if he goes to sea and sails on the account—
be it only for four or five days—must forget that there's ever
such a place as dry land. For a parish boy's life is a very frail
thing; and should he set foot on land he's as like as not to find
both feet dancing in the air. D'ye get my meaning, Jack?"

"Yes, sir," said I. "I should be hanged."

"Very good! Very good, indeed! So ye know all about the nubbing cheat?"

"Yes, sir. It's the Tree—the gallows."

"Capital, Jack! Really capital! Anyone with half an ear and eye could tell ye're a smart lad! I like ye, Jack! You and I will be well together! From yer wit I'll swear ye come from London. Is it so? Tell me, boy; for I like a London lad as well as any in the world!"

"I was found in Holborn, sir," said I, warming to his smiling mood.

"Found? Ah, yes, Morris told me: a foundling. Not to worry, Jack—with no name of yer own, ye've none to spoil, and none to be ashamed of. Was it a church door that mothered ye?"

"St Bride's, so I've been told, sir."

He looked at me very quizzically, then dropped his eyes again.

"Fourteen years ago, Jack? That's what ye told Morris."

"So I believe it was, sir."

There was a long pause in which he seemed to be debating with himself.

"It was thirteen, lad—take my word for it: it was thirteen years ago."

"W-why do you say that . . . sir . . . why?"

"Because—because ye *look* more thirteen than fourteen! There! Are ye satisfied?"

"Ye-es, sir . . . but . . . you paused—as if . . . as if you knew—remembered something—"

"I was thinking of something else."

"But you were looking at me—directly—as if—"

"—as if what?"

"I—I don't know—"

"As if I remembered something, ye said? What could I remember? A day, thirteen years ago? A lady, hooded, going to a church—maybe St Bride's? A lady whose face I knew? Even though she tried to hide it from the world? Is that it, Jack?"

"I don't know—I don't know!"

"A warm night, wasn't it? The month was—"

"July!"

"The month was July . . . the day—can I remember? maybe—maybe the fourteenth."

He muttered something which I didn't catch. I asked him what, but he laughed and shook his head. Then he stopped and looked at me with the most extraordinary seriousness so that the hot sun seemed to have grown suddenly cold.

"You look like your father, Jack. Very like."

I must have gone white as a ghost—for he seemed concerned and said he was sorry for what he'd said. He'd no wish to unsettle me. I was to forget it. So I got on my knees to him and begged him to tell me more "to forget". The name. The name. For God's sake, the name!

"His name is Death, Jack. He's dead."

"But my mother—"

To which he made answer that a parish boy is best off without such knowledge. Hadn't we agreed? It does no good to know such things. But I was afire to "be done no good to", and everything he said only fanned the flames. In moments I'd been transformed. The habitual gloom that had ever been at the centre of my life, dissolved. Considering the unfavourable circumstances that obtained, I was astonished with joy. The name! The name! It seemed impossible that he should hold off for long! I felt boundless powers of persuasion—I was irresistible. And he, plainly, was enchanted with me as I plagued him—only moving off a bit when I seemed likely to pluck at him: for he could never abide being touched . . . But he never moved far, so I was never discouraged.

I told him he *must* tell me. He laughed and told me "must" was a word I'd best forget. But he spoke kindly—not wanting to hurt—or offend. Then it turned out—God knows how!— he'd a great sense of justice and fair play. He'd a sense of *obligation*. If he'd been under *obligation* to me, he'd have given up my secret at once. But I was under *obligation* to him: twice. Twice

Mister Morris had saved me: once when I was first found, and a second time the morning after. And Mister Morris was his instrument. Therefore justice dictated—and fair play demanded —that I must first acquit myself of that double obligation, then lay a further one on him before it was reasonable to expect my secret.

So what was I to do? Nothing much. Only save his life three times. No more than that.

"Why! it might happen in a single day!" he exclaimed encouragingly, when he saw I looked somewhat crestfallen.

"I might slip—and you'd pull me back from drowning. A man might lose his wits and rush at me from behind—and you'd cry out or trip him: no fierce battle—which you'd lose—but just a word, or a well-placed foot to give me time, eh? You might even sniff out a promising betrayal . . . ye know the kind of thing, Jack: 'When the Devil goes ashore thou shine the beacon three times—as was fixed with the guards—'" Here he gave such a sly impersonation of Mister Taplow that, while none could have sworn to it, none could have missed it, neither. "So ye see, it's not such a hard bargain after all!"

"And if I do it?" My hopes soared as he made it sound so easy. (He could have made anything sound easy to me at that time. I was fire: I was light: I was the wind!)

"Upon the third saving, Jack—'Holborn' for the time being, eh?—upon the third saving I'll tell ye who ye really are. But— but don't blame me if ye're not satisfied, will ye, lad?"

He was on his feet and half-way up the companionway when I discovered myself to be running after him, shouting out very wildly, "A promise? A promise?"

"Save us from little boys! What a plague they are! Mister Morris! Come quick and save me from Jack! He'll worry me to death, I swear!"

The brisk little master appeared, as usual, from nowhere.

"Mister Morris, see that the lad is kept too busy to worry me. Why, we'd all go off our heads if children had their way!"

So at last I'd met him. And what a meeting! In the twinkling of an eye he'd given me what all my thirteen years had not: purpose; hope; almost certainty! *How* such a man had come to know my secret origin, I dared not guess. But he knew it. Of that, there was no doubt. Was it by supernatural means? I'd never believed in such things before—but then, it had never suited me to believe before. Maybe Mister Pobjoy was right? Maybe he *was* a kind of devil? But a very *kind* kind. I was in no mood to argue theology. All that mattered was that one man alive had my vital secret: that man was here and now: that man had fairly asked such and such of me in exchange— and I'd agreed. The outcome? Sometime, I'd know who I was. To which end I was to watch over him, be his extra eyes, ears, his extra sense without which he might go down.

One fine morning, three or four days following, Mister Pobjoy told me we were to make harbour that very night. "What harbour?" I asked him. "Wouldn't I like to know," he answered, and further comforted me with it "not being Bristol, nor Plymouth nor Southampton nor any other such place where a lad might be off and away and peach on his good kind mates for the lousy reward of a guinea. No: it was a quieter place than they: a wery private mouth come open in the bushy face of the shore—so small it scarcely whispered its presence to wessels that passed.

"And to all but its friends it whispered unheard. It was a place where coastguards might be caught napping; and them that dozed not might be found to wink . . . It was a place with an inn or two very willing to oblige a poor sailor by lightening the ballast of his pockets for the favour of never asking nor answering questions . . . It was a place of the Captain's, a particular place of his that he came to at particular times of the year for his own particular reasons. And the Devil knew what those reasons were."

I got my first glimpse of this secret place as the sun was setting abaft the starboard beam, making the poop all gold, and sweeping shadows of the masts and sails across the fore-castle. Then we rounded a brief headland and I saw the small mouth opening in the bushy shore, just as Mister Pobjoy had described.

We dropped anchor half a mile off shore and the longboat party was got ready. For a good while they stood, black as posts along the side, silent and waiting. I could hear sounds very plainly from the Captain's cabin. I think it was Mister Morris with him that night: Mister Morris who was always so close to him . . .

"And now for my hat, man! My hat and sword. That's it! That's it, eh?" (I fancied he looked in a mirror and was satisfied by what he saw.) "Yes—indeed, eh? That's—it!"

At last, he came out on deck, carrying a dark lantern. He was dressed in a full black coat and pale coloured breeches. I remember how the buttons glinted on his great cuffs as stray flickerings from the lantern caught them—and the coming and going of light on his thin sword . . . He wore a cocked hat somewhat slanting, and it gave him a rakish air, like a lord of the night.

He lifted his lantern and blinked it three times. Far away, in the direction of the now-hidden harbour, another light answered. Again he signalled. Again came the answer, uncannily prompt. He nodded, and one by one the shore party humped over the side and into the waiting boat. Last of all came—himself, and as he passed he seemed to smile. Of a sudden, his own words came back, and I found them uncomfortably apt: "When the Devil goes ashore, thou shine the beacon three times . . ." A very uneasy feeling seized me as I saw him rear up against the rail, then drop deftly down into the boat below. I looked hard for a last glimpse of his white face and cocked hat, but he and the boat was vanished into the night.

A very breathless night with no moon and a black blanket of a sky; mighty close, it seemed—as though we were shut away from Heaven for some purpose or other . . . A sheet,

23

hanging loose from the mainyard, began to smack gently against the mast: and such was the quiet that it sounded like a man being flogged. Then the distant sound of the longboat touching on shingle . . .

I think it must have been when the boat was not quite beached—secured, I mean—that there was disaster. Another minute might have accomplished more—

In the woods and undergrowth, an ambush had been waiting! Very quiet and deadly they'd lain there: watchful: eyes along musket-barrels: observing the little beach: breathing deep when the longboat came: counting footfalls on the shingle: patient: under cold orders—till one man, either from fright or eagerness, fired off his charge!

So they'd no choice but to abandon caution and burst out of hiding before the panic-struck men of the *Charming Molly* could scramble back into their boat! Those of them who'd been engaged in hauling, hopped and lay flat in the scuppers till the musket-fire was volleyed out. The others—the better half—were midway up the beach, so the onrush of the ambush cut them off. But for that too soon shot, not a soul would have got back to the boat.

Now began hand to hand fighting of the utmost fierceness and confusion. Cutlasses, knives, swords, nails and even teeth all set to work at once. The lost part of the crew scattered and fought ferociously to regain the longboat and, scratched, bitten, kicked and hacked-at, the ambushers pursued them in the tangled dark. Strange desperate duels were engaged, broke off, re-engaged with a shout, carried on across the tumbling pebbles and finished off in some squalid patch of black.

Then the ambushers re-formed and our men fought among themselves for a few seconds before they realised they'd got a slender chance. Those who could, fled: those who could not, lay like black starfish on the beach. One or two who lay close enough were dragged aboard the longboat, but the rest were past caring for, and with their last eyes watched all hope of salvation float panting and desperate out to sea. At last, the longboat scraped alongside and the shore party crept back aboard the amazed and silent ship.

I think it was when the longboat had dragged off the shore that I guessed—indeed, knew almost for a certainty—that something else had gone awry. A certain ragged aimlessness, an air of desolation hung over the shore, and on the orphaned boat itself, proclaiming something vital was gone.

I did not expect to see his face among those who heaved up over the rail. When he was not the first, I knew he could not be last: so there was no point in waiting.

I recalled the last glimpse I'd had of him: his white face under his cocked hat vanishing into the night—and I fell victim to that painful madness of trying to bring a moment back so's I could shout out and warn him, "Captain! You'll be killed! In five minutes! Come back!"

Then I heard Mister Morris sharply ordering men to stand aside—"Stand aside, there! Back! Back, d'you hear!"

Across the deck staggered the mildewed little master, under a burden he'd let no-one help him with. Very gentle and jealous he was; very careful of his precious burden, even though a great deal of blood kept running from it over his bursting arms, on to his breeches, striping his stockings . . . He'd let no man near him, nor say anything more than, "He's alive, I tell you . . . he's alive . . . he's alive . . ." over and over again. Mister Morris had brought back what was left of the Captain.

Chapter Four

HE lay very near to death. He'd been stabbed in the side and had lost much blood. Mister Morris mounted a guard over his cabin and let no-one pass inside. He himself took in the gruel Mister Pobjoy prepared, and brought out the bloody rags for me to wash. I got no closer to him than that.

In the calamity of that night (brought on by God knows what piece of bad luck or sour betrayal), there were lost ten men: nine killed ashore, and one that died aboard next morning of his wounds.

We sailed now on a westerly course, into the setting sun. The wind was small and from a-beam, so we went slow and the mists that came up at dawn rolled over us and seemed to shear the masts from the deck. These mists were heavy and wet, and when they'd gone they left the sails and rigging all dripping—as though the *Charming Molly* was weeping for her sick Captain.

"For a ship has a soul like a living thing," said Mister Pobjoy one morning as he ladled out the gruel. "Small wonder now she runs limp-sailed to a soldier's wind! She's no better than a widow left rudderless in the world with no-one to guide her—and no port to take her in."

There were tears in his red eyes, or something very like them.

"For Lord's sake, Mister Pobjoy!" I cried. "He's not dead yet! He's still alive . . . breathing . . . growing strong again . . ."

"Not dead . . . no, not dead . . ." He wiped his nose and looked about him eerily. "But his spirit's fading fast. Sometimes Pobjoy feels it in the shrouds, shifting to be free. And when it goes—ah! when those great wings flap away there'll be nothing between Pobjoy and the sky!"

His customary look of gin-soaked misery, or gin-hallowed peace, was gone off his face. Instead there was left the look of a very wretched old man, brooding frozenly on the meaning of what he'd said, wondering if his word was Fate and had set up a disaster in the future to which he needs must come . . .

"Here! Take this to him—if indeed he's still alive!"

He shivered and gave me the bowl which he'd absently overfilled.

His talk lay heavy on me as I went cautiously by the larboard rail; for the whiteness on deck was so thick that a man, three paces off, was no more than a shadow that might have been a mast.

I thought I saw the mizzen-mast straight ahead—and wondered how I'd come so far adrift. Then it went and I thought it might have been Sam Fox standing bolt upright, as he did these white mornings, as if he was waiting for someone . . .

I went very delicately, so's not to crash into him—if him it was—and lose the sick man's bowl. Then, very soft and faint, I could have sworn I heard a voice singing! I strained my ears, but the hundred different tongues of the *Charming Molly* all began whispering at once, and I could not be sure. Then I heard it maybe again—then not—not for many a long second—then once more, a snatch of it, very thin and far off:

> *"If I roam away*
> *I'll come back again*
> *Though I roam ten thousand miles . . ."*

I put out my hand to steady myself—and found that I was hard against the larboard rail. Which was very strange for the voice had come from my left where there was nothing but the empty sea . . .

I got to the quarter-deck without having heard it again, but my heart was pounding so violently that I shook with it and could scarce hold the gruel bowl steady. I'd had a bad fright and must have looked whiter than the mist, for Mister Morris stared at me queerly as he took the bowl and asked if I was sickening. (Since he'd been tending the Captain, he'd turned kinder, as if he'd caught a habit by it.)

"Is he better, Mister Morris?"

"Ye—es . . . but—"

I waited, very uneasy on that "but".

"He's lost a deal of blood and is very weak," finished up the master. "Most of the time he sleeps."

I was sure that wasn't what he began to say, for his "but"

still hung in the air between us. Nonetheless, there was nothing more to be got out of him.

So I went back toward the galley very sombrely thoughtful. Then the shadow of the mainmast came up sudden before me and I'd have stepped aside—when it dropped a great hand on my shoulder!

I saw it was Mister Taplow, scowling and screwing up his eyes against the vapours. He must have watched me go aft with the gruel and waited for my return.

"Is he dead, Jack? Is he dead?"

"He's sleeping, Mister Taplow."

"Did see him, then?"

"Mister Morris told me—"

"Lies! He's dead and Morris sails for a ghost!"

"That's not so! He's alive—"

"Dead! Dead! Dead! Dead as granite! Dead as iron! Dead as stinking pitch!"

"He's alive, I tell you!" Suddenly, the Captain's life seemed held between his desire and my hope.

"And I say he's not!" He hammered in his words like nails. "D'you not know the feel of a ship when there's a corpse aboard? How she reeks like a coffin and goes like a hearse?"

Sam Fox came out of the mist, drawn by the sound of our voices. He was with Mister Taplow, and the three of us stood together, wishing away, willing away, struggling to hold on to the soul of that evil man who lay in his cabin.

"He's gone! The ship stinks of death!"

"You're mistook! He's lost much blood and sleeps—"

"Aye! We all know that sleep. And I'll tell thee another thing—"

But he never did. He stopped and we stood very quiet while out of the mist came that queer voice singing again:

"*If I roam away*
I'll come back again
Though I roam ten thousand miles . . ."

"There it is again," breathed Sam Fox; and he and Mister Taplow stared at me as if I'd called a spirit from the deep. They went to the rail and searched the shifting whiteness.

"What was that?"

"Shadow of the mainmast."

"D'ye hear anything?"

"No. It's gone!"

"Hark!"

Very soft, it came once more: "*Though—I—roam—ten—thousand—miles* . . . ."

"Where was it?"

"Over there!"

"What? Aloft?"

"How the Devil can I see in this damned vaporous air?"

"Look! Look! It's growing lighter! It's lifting!"

It must have been close on midday, for the top of the mist was turning to gold and the great yellow sun came rolling and melting out of it. Out to sea the billowing whiteness began to shiver and be drawn up, like a playhouse curtain, and there lay the grey waters again, glittering in the sun. Now was the crew all born again—and we were no more alone by the larboard rail.

Every man aboard seemed alongside of us, staring for the Devil knew what. Some had pistols and muskets, some knives and some nothing but their clenched fists and starting eyes.

"Look, boys, look! Three-quarters aft! Fifty yards off! D'ye see it? There now! There it goes!"

For a moment, I thought it was a man standing on the water; then a coil of vaporous air shivered away and I saw he was on a raft. Just one single man standing frailly out there, waving to us and singing for joy at being rescued:

> "*If I roam away*
> *I'll come back again*
> *Though I roam ten thousand miles!*"

I don't know whether I was more glad than mad to've been

cheated out of a ghost; but one of the crew was in no two minds about it. He loosed off a musket and sent a ball tearing up the water a yard off the raft.

"You've done with your perishing roaming now, m'lad!"

This set on some dozen of the others who began taking cheap shots at the poor wretch.

The clapping and rattle of musketry was a very ironical sound to greet a song: a very sickening and abominable sound, for the man on the raft had nothing to defend himself with, nor no sail with which to escape: and he'd done his murderers no more harm than maybe frightening them a bit by his singing in the mist . . . Even the sensible, dapper Mister Morris was come out onto the poop-deck and stood watching, pleasantly: then he went back to tell the Captain of the morning's sport.

I tried to wave in hope he'd see me and know—before he was killed—that there was one aboard who wished him no harm. But he missed it, for his head was buried in a bundle of dark cloth. So I gave up looking as I'd no desire to watch him hit, and waited for the shout of joy and triumph that would mark his end. Three or four more shots I heard, then a voice cried out:

"Stop, lads! Stop! Look at that!"

There was a rough kind of mast on the raft, and on this he'd managed to hang a flag. It fluttered out—black, with a white death's head.

"He's one of us, boys! He's on the account!"

"He's one of us!" Wonderful, wonderful! Maybe another Mister Taplow—or a substitute for Ben Fox. Exactly what the world most needed! And I'd pitied him!—Cheered almost aloud when the bullets kept missing him. Now I knew why they had: he'd been born to be hanged, not shot. He'd got my pity under false pretences; doubtless, in his time, he'd got many things that way, but pity rankled most. It was a great indignity and I wished him dead for it.

But he lived, so I made the best of it by reflecting he'd be a fresh face among the stale, and, though he might be no better than my daily companions, it wasn't possible he could be worse.

Shortly after, he came aboard with enough ceremony to've been King Neptune. I never saw so many helping hands—on so many murderers' arms.

I tried to get a look at him: but there was no hole in the crowd.

Then as the crowd shifted to let Mister Morris through, I caught sight of waving dark hair and a pair of shrewd brown eyes that seemed to be quizzing new friends—and old, disagreeable faces. Then ragged backs came between and I turned to go back to my home in the galley—to share my feelings with Mister Pobjoy.

The galley was empty. Mister Pobjoy had gone out on deck. Filth and confusion was everywhere—as was usual. He never did a thing to clean up. Then I remembered, he'd told me to do it. "Jack's job . . . get down to it . . . Jack's job!"

I banged about a good deal as I worked, for I was growing angrier by the second. Everything conspired to make me worse: small disasters came like an avalanche . . . I ran a splinter off a pork barrel into my thumb; which made me drop a mug slap into the brine.

"Rot him for coming aboard!" (I meant the stranger—that musical Neptune). I plunged my sore fist in after the mug and the salt stung my wound murderously. So I whipped out my fist—and got another splinter in the tenderest part of my arm—the underside of the elbow, just above the crook.

"Rot Mister Pobjoy and his filthy ways! Rot this foul ship and her foul crew! And rot the day that ever I went to sea!"

I sat back and wiped my burning hands across my face. The salt went straight to my eyes and I thought I was sent to Hell.

I crouched, with my hands before my face and everything forgot in salty misery . . .

And then a very queer thing happened. A hand was laid lightly on my shoulder.

"Who's there?" I whispered. For answer, I felt the fingers grip into me—and then the hand was gone. When I could open my eyes, there was no-one by. I ran to look outside. There was no-one near. I went back to the galley and found, on the boards behind where I'd crouched, some drops of fresh blood.

The Captain! It must have been he! The fresh blood . . . the effort of walking must have re-opened his wound. Only a few drops. Thank God it wasn't more! The morning's commotion must have roused him. He'd come out to see. And now was gone again? Why? Didn't he care for what he saw? God knew! He'd laid his hand on my shoulder and that was enough! The world became suddenly a remarkable fair place again.

When the mildewed little sailing-master came in at last with the draggled catch from the morning's sea—for to feed him or some such worthwhile thing—I was in such a state of excitement I couldn't have told if he'd one head or two. And this was the stranger who, not half an hour before, had filled all my thoughts. Six drops of blood had washed him clean from my mind.

Chapter Five

I SLEPT badly that night: the strange commotions of the day had set my brain in a stew. A dozen times I thought I heard someone limping about in the dark; so I got up, looked outside to the quiet deck and the quiet sky—and the watch, still as

C

stone on the forecastle head. There was never any more than
that. Of the Captain there was never a sign. So back I'd go to
Mister Pobjoy: (Mister Pobjoy, quarter awake and cursing
like mad for it).

Next day on deck, all was clear sunshine and sharp shadows:
the mists were left behind and the sky was clear—save for a
small grey hump on the horizon behind us. But the shadows
somehow kept shifting past the corners of my eyes and I
couldn't take two paces without stopping to see what had
stirred.

All that day he haunted me like a half-remembered dream;
till I began to think that's all he'd been—no more than the
weary residue of a bad night: the effect of too little sleep on a
too little brain. Then, towards nightfall, I felt his presence
depart and I knew I'd not been mistaken. The shadows, though
deeper, were now dead; and I saw the lamp lit in his cabin.
He'd abandoned whatever he'd been seeking.

But why had he secretly left his cabin? What had brought
him out? Only one thing. The stranger. What was there about
this man who'd seemed so ordinary to me I'd even forgot his
face? What was he to the Captain to've drawn him from his
sickbed so secretly and warily . . . ? Something disquieting
and strange.

That night I had recourse to Mister Pobjoy again, who
seemed to know so much of the inside of things even though
he saw them through the bottom of a cup of gin. He'd not
seen much more of the stranger than I had; for that mysterious gentleman had been dozing in some hidden corner all
day, following his ordeal by sea. Yet he'd seen enough of his
outside to surmise at his inside, and heard enough of his history
to guess at the truth of it.

"Bless you, Mister Pobjoy!" said I. "But what's become of
our shipwrecked gentleman?"

"Shipwrecked?" quoth he. "Saved from the horrible briny?
Set on a convenient raft by a dolphin (who helped him rig
a mast)? And all his clothing handed out to him by the ghostly

arm of a drowned mate who thought he might need it henceforward? No, dear boy, Mister Solomon Trumpet was never
shipwrecked! Why, bless you! He was put adrift: cast off!
Abandoned even as thou wast in thine pitiful infancy. Only—
only—(unless thou was the most forward brat that ever saw
light in London), *thou* wasn't abandoned for—mutiny!"

"What manner of man is he?" I asked uneasily.

"A wery bad mannered man—discontented like all muti-
neers. A man wery disposed to work on others: and quick to
do none himself." (From which, I gathered, he'd offered no
help to Mister Pobjoy when it had been canvassed.)

"What kind of vessel did he come off, Mister Pobjoy?"

"A wery *kind* kind of wessel: kind to cast him off instead of
slitting his glib little throat!"

Then shrewd, mysterious Mister Pobjoy, who'd sorted out
all he'd known and heard of, and who smelled with amazing
sharpness which way an ill wind blew, told me a tale of a ship
called the *Esperance*. I'd never heard of her; but Mister Pobjoy
had, and Mister Taplow had—and so had many another such
desperate dreamer.

Two years before, she'd sailed from Plymouth with a cargo
of strong spirits, old muskets and cheap beads. She'd sailed to
the Devil knew where and traded her cargo for a huge treasure
of gold and jewels. Filled up her hold with it. Sailed so low
in the water thereafter that she was never seen from more than
half a mile.

Some said she was in the Indian Ocean; some said she was
in Virginian waters; some said she was rounding the Cape of
Storms; and some said she was at the bottom of the sea, with
all her crew disposed as skeleton millionaires. But the truth of
the matter was otherwise . . . She was creeping back home.

"A ripe plum is the *Esperance*: a fat ripe plum indeed. But
in this plum grew a maggot—a shrewd, nipping little maggot
with eyes as quick as corks!"

Here Mister Pobjoy spat and squashed his thumb down on
the board—as was his practice with maggots.

Now he went on to tell of disaster aboard the *Esperance*; of discontent and greed: of plunder, and murder, and mutiny on mutiny as the huge treasure moaned to be stole and spent. He told of hangings and stabbings and quick buryings at sea; of bitter arguings, and desperate shiftings of power; and of the little maggot that nipped from side to side—ever increasing its share of the plum by stirring up bloodshed . . . never on any side but its own . . . till at last, either by bad luck or bad judgement, it was hooked out squirming into the angry light of day.

"Why didn't they kill him?" I burst in, and Mister Pobjoy looked honestly puzzled:

"It's wery hard to find any reason for not doing in a man," he said, at length.

"And—and he told—all this—?"

"Bless you, not with his tongue! With his slippery eyes and thieving fingers! And with his swivelling looks! What was told with his *tongue* the Devil knows! Best ask whoever listened. But most was deafened when they heard mention of the *Esperance*. A wery powerful earstopper, that!"

Then, with a cheerful injunction not to wake him this night like the last, lest he slit my dear throat with a pork-knife, he slopped off to bed, emptied of talk and full of gin.

In vast excitement I lay and brooded on the character and inclinations of Mister Solomon Trumpet. Mister Pobjoy I never doubted. None had a keener nose than he for evil: and he was always sniffing. He sniffed even in his sleep, as if his dreams were suspect.

Now I understood what had been meant by the hand on my shoulder. "Wake up, Jack! I'm putting ye in the way of redeeming the promise! With a quick wit ye might save my life! Watch—this—fellow—Trumpet for me."

I met him next morning by the larboard rail. I was on my way from Mister Morris, carrying an empty bowl, and he was leaning, negligently, with his back to the sea, watching me as I came.

"Good morning, Jack, old son."

I marked him well. He was slender and a little below the general in height and neatly dressed in plain brown cloth. His complexion was smooth and rosy, with lively red lips and crooked brown eyes that had little pouches like money-bags hung beneath them. These grew fat and full when he smiled. "Good morning, I said."

I never answered, but continued on my way, looking back only before I turned into the galley. He was still by the rail, but now looking out to sea. Very intently. I thought I knew what for. His eyes were bright with longing.

When next I'd occasion to come out—to empty a pair of pails—he'd moved toward the quarterdeck. He was talking to Mister Morris . . . very eagerly . . . gesturing . . . pointing . . . shrugging, and shaking his head . . . staring up to the topsails— or to Heaven—then down to Mister Morris's cold eyes . . . Mister Morris, nearly dapper little gentleman, shook his head and would have turned away; but Mister Trumpet seemed eternally before him. I tried to get nearer, but I saw Mister Trumpet's nose wrinkle as the perfume from my pails reached him. Then Mister Morris turned on his heel and went away. Mister Trumpet stared after him, till he felt my intent watching. He swung about with a long, crooked, questioning look that was seasoned with bitterness. But I'd seen the look it had so swiftly replaced: desperation and rage.

I began to back away when one of my pails caught against something—tipped and spilled. I turned to see what had been unlucky. Mister Taplow! A pint of Mister Pobjoy's stinking waste ran down his breeches. But there wasn't any rage on his face, though his huge fists were clenched as if to pound my head in. They hung at his sides as if forgot.

He was looking over the top of me. His mouth, still open to curse, widened into a kind of smile. Mister Trumpet, by the quarterdeck, smiled back—into Mister Taplow's hot eyes.

A quick smile, hid the instant it showed. Mister Taplow wiped his fist across his mouth, opening his fingers as he did so, his great forefinger loitering by his nose then tracing a slow line down by the side of his mouth as if to draw a new shape for it...

Toward afternoon the weather grew sweatily hot and the wind dropped to near nothing. Despite the great heat, Mister Morris had the crew swarming along the yards to fix every inch of canvas we possessed to catch the dying wind. Under full sail, the *Charming Molly* flapped and creaked and groaned like an old man at his exercise; and, like an old man, made little headway owing to a most pitiful lack of wind.

The faint grey hump I'd seen on the horizon behind us was now grown into a little mountain that seemed to join the sea with the sky. Whatever it was, it drew continual uneasy looks from every man aboard and drove them to the task of making good speed to outpace it. There was but one opinion of that blackness: "God help us if we get into it!"

Then the sun climbed slowly across and down over our jib, where it hung like a bloody lamp. Great black and purple clouds crept up in the sky behind us, in crazy, frightening shapes. Most often they were like wild beasts with outflung claws—and I kept recalling some words I'd heard: "There she goes, like a great black tiger in the sky."

I'd not seen Mister Trumpet for some hours, and toward evening, Mister Taplow, likewise, disappeared. I began to look in all the dark corners. But there was never a sign of Mister Trumpet or Mister Taplow. One place alone remained to be searched; but for that I had to wait till night. When it was dark, I went there and prayed no light would betray me as I inched back the hatch. I'd an idea Mister Trumpet and Mister Taplow were foregathered in the hold.

A most absolute silence reigned within, and all the old familiar stench rose quietly up, like a blind thing questioning. For a moment, I thought I was wrong—or I'd alarmed them by some movement—then slight sounds began to be heard. One by one I recalled them: the creak of the bulwarks complaining

... the slap of the waves on our sides ... the gentle swosh of bilge in our scuppers ... the womanish rustle of frantic rats ... But there was another sound also, a faint hissing that came and went, came and went ... A sound of breathing.

"What was that?"

Men's whispers are hard to recognize. Passion and concealment make them alike. But I thought it was Mister Taplow.

"Must have been a rat!"

The silence was extraordinarily long, and all the familiar sounds died away out of respect for it.

"It's quiet now."

That was Mister Trumpet. I could have sworn he laid his hand on Mister Taplow's arm: "Old friend, there's not much time left."

I heard the other let out his breath as if it pained him. Then Mister Trumpet resumed what he'd been up to—which was the tempting of Taplow with the treasure of the *Esperance*.

I could hear Mister Taplow's breath coming fiercer, as if it tore him as it came.

Now there appeared a sting in Mister Trumpet's words—a very inward poison that ate him up with bitterness against Mister Morris and the Captain he'd never seen. For they'd have none of his plan, so ten million pounds in gold and jewels was slipping quickly through his grasp.

He'd told how rich the *Esperance* was, but his answer had been, "Wealth isn't everything in this world."

("Aye, there's beggary, too, old friend!") He'd promised she was unarmed—sworn to it—and had been told "The coming storm had ball and shot for two. Escape the storm and live to fight another day."

("Live to fight? What kind of life with nothing in our pockets but regret?")

So he ran on till Mister Morris and the Captain were torn to shreds of cautious cowardice—"little men, little men on the account ... but of small account ... too small to cast a shadow on the golden dream that sailed so close ..."

Mister Taplow sucked in the corrupting poison with every breath he drew. As the foul air went into his lungs, I felt him being puffed up into an enormous semblance of Mister Trumpet's wicked desires.

"And she's for certain unarmed, d'you swear?"

"Not enough powder to dab on the nose of our *Molly*!"

"And all else—?"

"—Is as I said!"

"THEN I'LL DO IT!"

The words fell like hammer-blows and seemed to shake the ship from stem to stern. I thought they were done. I thought even Mister Trumpet was startled at the violence of the monster he fancied he'd made. And maybe he was. For there came now another, queerer side to Mister Trumpet's nature. Mister Taplow was committed—but his tempter wriggled away. He wondered at the danger of it. He feared his "old friend" might be betrayed before anything was achieved. He begged caught Mister Taplow to reconsider before he took his fatal step. If I'd not heard what had gone before, I'd have sworn he was against the Welshman, striving by reason to stop him. But somehow his words lit fiercer fires than ever before—and Mister Taplow was fairly gasping in the heat of them. Opposing had strengthened him, tested out his weaknesses and let the fires within flame out and seal them up.

"Till tomorrow, then?"

"At noon. Be by the quarterdeck."

"The signal?"

"I've told you!"

"I cannot agree."

"Much I care!"

"Change it!"

Yes—change it, good Mister Taplow! Speak up so's Jack can hear! Change it for my dear sake! For I can't hold on much longer! I'd a strong desire to sneeze, coupled with a sudden, violent itch demanding to be scratched—and the ladder rung bit into my hands till I thought my fingers would be sliced off.

But Mister Taplow would not change the signal. Urgently, Mister Trumpet tried him—but, as before, opposing only made him the more adamant. I thought Mister Trumpet was genuine in his misliking of the signal—and was now reaping the reward of his own cunning. He could do nothing. To all his entreaties came Mister Taplow's violent, grating, "No!"

"I beg you—while there's time—"

But there *was* no time. It was run out. Above, Mister Morris had begun to curse and shout and rout out his missing men. The storm canvas was to be put up.

"Suckling! Clark! Taplow! Jack! On deck! All hands on deck! I'll chop off any pair seen idle! Taplow! Taplow, I say!"

I fled up into the hurly-burly on deck. God knows whether I was heard or seen. I didn't think so—for there was the Devil to pay and a confusion of haste. Mister Morris was everywhere.

"The storm! The storm!" he kept shouting—"Hurry! Get 'em up before the storm!"

But he was too late. I knew he was too late. The storm had already broke—in Mister Taplow's heart.

Chapter Six

A busy, frantic night with the deck like a street market, draped and piled with the vast yardage of canvas. Every man aboard (save Mister Trumpet) was lashing and lugging and hoisting and belaying till the sweat ran down in pools and steamed up off the deck. The wind was quite gone, and there being no movement in the air, all grew stale with expelled breath till the *Charming Molly* was blanketed in the waste of gasping lungs.

Close on midnight, I began to feel faint and sick and had to go and lean over the side. The light of our lanterns showed we still crept along, though so slow we made no more stir than a thick, sluggish ripple which rolled continuously off our bows like an endless black worm . . .

I went off to the galley to lie down awhile—and was surprised to be visited by Mister Trumpet. He stood in the doorway, watching me.

"What d'you want, Mister Trumpet?"

He hesitated. "D'you—d'you say no prayers before you sleep, old fellow?"

"I'm a foundling," said I. "There's none who taught me how."

"Why, it's easy! Just on your knees and your palms together and address yourself to Heaven in a humble voice. No more than that!"

"Why must it be so?"

"A custom, old son: just as one uncovers to a lady, or stands for the King. A custom that shows respect, so to speak."

"And what shall I pray for?"

"Why—as you're alone, old friend, pray for yourself! Ask for mercy on your soul. Commend it to the Lord, as the saying goes. It'll never come amiss!"

I fell asleep as soon as he'd gone and dreamed all night of the signal. First it was one thing, then another. A nod from Mister Clark; a wink from Sam Fox; a spit from Mister Taplow; Mister Trumpet blowing his nose . . . In my dream I flew from spot to spot—and always something happened behind me. Men would come up in front of me, pluck me by the arm and cry: "Clark winked, Jack! What's it to thee?"

"Sam Fox nodded, Jack! What's it to thee?"

Then I'd whip round to be told: "Taplow spat, Jack—behind thee!"

"Mister Trumpet blew his nose, Jack—behind thee!"

I must have whirled round a hundred times, for when I

woke, the nest of rags that served me for a bed was wrapped round me like a winding-sheet.

"Too many bellies," grunted Mister Pobjoy, when the last of the crew had come and gone with his stint of food. "Them or this storm'll be the end of this perishing wessel."

On deck, all was lashed secure and the patched storm-canvas hung dismally from the yards. Everywhere, men stood, leaned and clung silently, for there was nothing more to be done till the weather broke. Ragged and black against the canvas and sky, they hung in the shrouds and on the yards, moving no more than the hanging sails. There was not even the scream of gulls any more, for the sea was emptied of all save us under the gloomy, dreadful sky.

Mister Trumpet was at the larboard rail, wrapped up in a study of the flat, oily-looking sea. But the *Esperance*, wherever she might have been, kept out of our sight.

Then the Dutchman up in the crosstrees cried out: "A sail! A sail!" and for a while there was excitement, till, stare as they might, no-one else saw it and even the Dutchman called down, "Very far off! Low in de wasser! Goink now! Goink! Nein! Nothink! Nil!"

Mister Taplow stood just forward of the mainmast, with one great hand on a halyard. Had the sight of a sail been the signal? He never stirred. Mister Trumpet was to go to the quarterdeck. That much I'd heard. But was it before the signal—or after it? Mister Trumpet never stirred neither: only he glanced up to the Dutchman when he'd shouted, and then looked back over the larboard bow. The signal was yet to come.

"Der sail again!" called the Dutchman—and Mister Morris put up his glass and searched the larboard horizon.

"I see it now!" cried Mister Trumpet, moving to find a better vantage point.

But now three or four others saw it, and for the moment the ominous sky was forgot. I was standing not far from the forecastle on the larboard side, and was watching Mister

43

Taplow till my eyes were nearly falling out. I couldn't see all of him, for the mainmast was between us, but I could see his great hand still on the halyard and the sleeve of his faded red-striped shirt flutter: for a faint breeze had begun to blow.

Cautiously, the sails moved away from the masts, crackling and flapping as the deep creases were jerked out of them. Mister Taplow's grip on the halyard shifted. I moved round to get a better look at him. The wind came and went fitfully, making a sighing sound as it swept through the rigging. For an instant, a nearly white sun flew out of the dark. It was directly overhead. Noon.

Noon! Where was Mister Trumpet now? He was gone close to the quarter-deck. Still Mister Taplow never moved. The signal must come soon. He'd picked a good time. Every man's eye was fixed on the billowing of the great black cloud. It seemed even Heaven was on his side. I began to move aft, to get between Mister Taplow and the poop.

Every man's eyes were on the cloud; save Mister Clark's! *He* was watching me. Straddled across his fat cannon, he watched me as I went. I got a sick feeling he'd been watching me for some time now. I passed by him, and his pale blue eyes glittered as they shifted: then I heard him slide off his mount. I stopped to see if he'd follow.

Suddenly, I saw Mister Taplow, his hand still on the halyard, watching Mister Clark. What was the signal? I turned to look at Mister Clark. He was standing by his cannon, staring at me. My shirt felt cold and wet against my back. I was sweating like mad. A sound of bare feet landing softly on the deck made me turn. Sam Fox stood ahead of me. Still Mister Taplow never moved—but turned his eyes to Mister Fox.

The wind was no longer fitful, but blew steadily, with growing force.

Sam Fox began to move towards me. Mister Taplow's eyes shifted. What was the signal? I tried to pass round Mister Fox— but Mister Clark had moved to cut me off. I tried the other

44

way, but Sam Fox moved in closer. Even yet Mister Taplow leaned on the halyard; but his eyes were alive with excitement.

I looked to the quarter-deck, suddenly desperate to catch Mister Morris's eye: but he, like the rest, was intent on the tremendous cloud. Slowly I was being forced back on the rail. "For pity's sake, Mister Morris, look this way! Leave the hell in the sky and spare a glance for the hell down here!"

I saw Mister Trumpet. He was staring at me with a look of horrified compassion. As I looked, he seemed to spread his hands and shake his head. Too late, I knew what the signal was to be. A death. Mine!

His curious lips moved as if to say, "Not my fault, old son—tried to change the signal—did what I could—made you pray for your soul—your blood's not on my hands—"

"Mister Morris! Mister Morris!" But the wind had begun to howl and my words were whipped away. Mister Fox, with his black hair all stretched forward in the gale, spread his arms to catch me if I should run. Mister Clark, beside him, did likewise. Together they came at me, tilting with the deck.

No more than a yard lay between us when the Dutchman saw the sail again. "Yonder! Yonder! Der sail!"

For an instant, they paused. I made a run for it and crashed past an outstretched hand. I felt fingers (Sam Fox's, I think), scrape through my hair—and I left him holding a fistful of it!

Mister Taplow was gone from the halyard! I flew toward the quarter-deck for Mister Morris. He lay stunned at the foot of the companionway. I began to mount when Mister Trumpet grabbed me by the shoulder.

"Leave 'em be! Leave 'em be! Enough that you've escaped! Don't try to stop it now! You can't—and they'll do for you!"

I shook free and crawled upward. I'd glimpsed a rag of red and white striped shirt above me. I was almost on the quarter-deck, yelling, "Taplow! Taplow!"

He heard me and looked down. His mad face against the mad sky stopped me in my tracks. He was the living image of the storm.

"Taplow!"

His head jerked back and his great naked foot swung over to crash me on the head. I seized him by the ankle and was lifted clear off my foothold. For a second, I swung, then I dug my teeth into his bitter heel.

He must have released his hold above to free himself from me—for I remember no more than his roar of sharp pain—then both of us, my teeth still in him—crashing to the deck below.

Chapter Seven

To all you gentlemen who cannot sleep, whether from heat, cold, dread, expectation, pain or a gloomy conscience, let me give you a certain remedy: a fall of ten feet onto a wooden deck, head first. With a huge Welshman on top of you it's more sure, of course; but if one's not to hand you'll sleep quite sound from your own progress alone. I promise you.

True, your brain will be shook up a bit by the remedy of the deck and loose a few queer dreams into your snoozing . . . for it won't be all blackness . . . Faces will come and go, and faraway voices telling you to "Lie easy . . . spread your sails . . . you're coming to fair weather, lad . . . the storm's behind you now . . ." but who speaks, you'll never know, nor even care very much; it will all sound like idle nonsense and not be troubled over by a dozing brain.

Who tends you, who lays cold cloths on your hot head, whose capable gentle hands ease you back onto the bunk when the rolling sea would have pitched you off, you'll never know either. Maybe it was Mister Morris: maybe it was the man in the moon.

47

So, added to all the other benefits from this kind of sleep, you're even spared the labour of being grateful for the saving of your life. The only thing I'll say against it is, that four and twenty hours or more are gone from your life like a torn-out page; and something in them has bequeathed you a pain like a deck-board being left to bang about inside of your head.

So I slept. I slept and the world went on without me—and neither of us cared very much what became of the other. When I awoke, both me and the *Charming Molly* were blown a vast way off our course, and I never knew where I was till Mister Pobjoy brought me some broth that was half sea water and told me I was in Mister Morris's cabin. His face was blotched with purple from the lashing of wind and sea, and his poor beard was washed free of every living thing.

A very wet and wretched Mister Pobjoy who came and squashed down beside me in a reeking pool of sea. A very lonely Mister Pobjoy who'd none to share his galley now; and a very curious, uneasy Mister Pobjoy whose little eyes kept running round the cabin as if frantic thoughts (not his own) were chasing them . . .

"He knows him, Jack!"

He put his face so close to mine there wasn't room for a thought between us.

"He knows him, Jack!"

"Who?" I breathed, trying to blow him off.

He sat back, rubbed the side of his nose and pulled at his ear. "What have ye heard, Jack?"

"Nothing but the wind."

"What d'ye know, Jack?"

"Nothing but what Mister Pobjoy chooses to tell."

He sighed: "Bless you, dear boy, Pobjoy's choice is compulsion. He *must* tell you—else he'll burst and there'll be nothing left of him save a strange tale whirling in the wind and haunting the shrouds o' nights."

His tale began with a roar and a bang: the roar was Mister Taplow's; the bang was mine as my head hit the deck.

He'd come wild from the galley thinking, "the wessel had foundered", then he saw me "roll limp as a rag down the deck". My head was painted with blood, which afterward turned out to be from Mister Taplow's heel which I'd "bitten wery wenomously and might have died of it". But at first he'd thought the blood was mine and I was dead.

Indeed, he'd said to Suckling, " 'Mister Suckling, let this sad *Molly* bury him now, decent and quick. For he's dead as mutton.' In the meanwhile, Mister Morris had come out of his swoon in a flaming rage, and, with a gill of blood (his own) running down his face, was kicking pore Mister Taplow wery wiciously as if to stove in his ribs at the expense of a boot. But Mister Taplow, peaceful as an angel, never felt a thing. In which lies a moral, dear boy—never spend wenom on an unconscious man; for it's labour gone to waste."

Now came the part that was strange; the part that had haunted Mister Pobjoy and drove him from his peace and sleep and soured his very gin. . . .

"None saw the Captain's door open; but one minute there was nothing, and the next, *he* stood on the quarter-deck as if come out of the air. Wery white in the face, he was, drained dry, leaning on his stick, screwing up his eyes against the light they was strangers to: a ghost of the man that was!

"He stood and stared, and Mister Morris desists from kicking Mister Taplow, and the Dutchman holds up your pore self as if apologising for your being so small . . ."

Here Mister Pobjoy blinked hard several times as if he was come to the particular part.

"He was going to say something to Mister Morris when he stopped, still as a stone—with the great wind whipping at every movable part of him. He was looking at Mister Solomon Trumpet. And Mister Trumpet was looking up at him. Rooted. Opened and shut his mouth as if all the air in the world wasn't enough to bring back his breath. White as a bone. And the Captain? Red as fire! Not a word spoke—save by their eyes. And none knew what *they* said! But they spoke wolumes—if only a man might have read 'em!

"Then the Captain dropped his gaze and limped quickly back whence he'd come. But Mister Trumpet never stirred—never breathed, maybe—for close on a quarter of an hour. Nothing turned him from his staring at where the Captain had stood: neither the carrying of your goodself nearly under his nose, nor the dragging off of pore Taplow by three kind friends to be chained to the mainmast down in the hold. He stared and stared as if the Captain still occupied the wacant air—and was a sight as sudden and horrible as ever a man did see."

His voice died away and he, too, crouched staring into the vacant air as if the scene was still before him. "Horrible . . ." he mumbled, but it was more of a question than a memory. Then, as the sound of the wind and sea filled the cabin, he mumbled again, "Like a wild beast . . ." But I think he must have meant another sound, pitched to pierce the storm: a sound like the mainsail being torn slowly across: a hoarse, retching, howling sound.

"Taplow," he said, "Pore, mad Taplow—fighting his chains in the hold. Hark, and ye can hear them jangle . . ."

So I listened and my broth got stone-cold.

When he rolled away back to his galley, he left me profoundly disturbed.

"He knows him, Jack!" But in what way? It must have been an extraordinary acquaintance to shake them so! No words: nothing but amazement. How had they met before? What lay between them? "A sight as sudden and horrible as ever a man did see."

"A blackguard! A monster!" Another visitor, come to cheer me. "The worst thing in all the world! Guard yourself, old son! Guard yourself against him!"

Mister Trumpet. Crept in while I brooded, and his subtle voice broke in on my thoughts.

"Cut free and change sides—before it's too late."

He bent close to me and went on urging and urging till my head ached worse than ever, trying to remember which voice I was listening to—his present one, or the one that had tempted Mister Taplow in the hold. I wondered he wasn't in irons: and then I recalled I was the only one who'd overheard him. So I had power over him. I tried to catch his eye, but his look was too quick and slippery and full of fears and passions . . .

I was going to tell him he'd best watch his step, because he was in my power and I'd not hesitate to inform on him— when he looked outside and grew suddenly stiff. He turned back to me, his eyes fairly blazing. His lips seemed to move, but to no purpose, then he was pushed curtly aside.

At last it was the Captain! Lord, but he was white! His country complexion was all drained away. How little blood there must have been left in him!

"Awake? Awake, lad?" But his voice was good to hear as ever. "Yer eyes are bright as stars!"

Leaning heavily on his stick, he tapped his way perilously across the swinging cabin and laid his hand on my head. "Not a flicker of fever, yet they're bright as stars!"

He'd not sit beside me as I'd half-expected him to do— remembering how easily he'd once squatted beside me on the deck.

"I'll not stay long. I'll not tire ye. When I was sick in me cabin I was glad of peace and quiet. And ye must be likewise, eh? I just looked in to thank ye, Jack, for saving me life. Thank ye—thank ye. Ye've laid a great burden on me and I must acquit myself before final sentence is passed."

He was moving about all the time as if there was an awkwardness between us that never was before. Plainly, he would be gone. But I'd saved his life. That's what mattered.

"Then you'll remember, sir," said I with great hopefulness, "that I *have* saved you this once?"

He gave me such a look I wished I'd never spoke. His

fish-like eyes drove into my very soul with something like
contempt. But one of us had to keep the score . . .

"I'll remember, boy, for it's not my practice to forget."

Next morning (though it was black as night), Mister Morris,
who'd a bloody rag round his head, woke me and told me
I was better. Gone were my hopes of remaining his guest.
He never said a word of what I'd done: he saw I was alive and
jerked his thumb to the swinging door. Back whence I'd come:
back where I belonged: back to Mister Pobjoy's galley. The
wound was healed and I was once more Mister Pobjoy's scab.

So nothing remained of the mutiny save Mister Taplow,
chained to the mainmast in the hold. And there wasn't overmuch of him left—for he was gone raving mad with the dark
and his ruined hopes. Then he went entirely, in a quietly
sinister way.

When Mister Pobjoy opened the hatch to fling down his
food, he saw he was dead; and with a marlin-spike clean
through his back. Who had done this thing seemed no vast
mystery. Previously, the Captain had sent word to Taplow
to bid him stop his howling before he stopped it himself.
Now he howled no more. So there was peace in the hold—
but precious little anywhere else.

Chapter Eight

WE buried Mister Taplow two days after he died. Before that
the weather had been too fierce, and we heaved and rolled so
much that it would have been impossible to've brought up
a heavy thing like the Welshman's body from the hold. But
sometime, Mister Pobjoy had been down to "lay him out",

and sew him into a rough kind of sacking shroud "out of respect and decency for the pore murdered dead" (I wondered whose idea it had been: the simple Mister Pobjoy's, or the deep-down scheming one's?).

During those two days, nothing was said of the murder.

But if nothing was uttered, much was thought. I never knew the *Charming Molly* to be so patched with silences. For certain-sure Mister Taplow deserved what he got. But not in the back; and chained up the while. A man such as Mister Taplow deserved to see his end approach—and be able to prepare for it . . . not in the dark, and in the back . . .

These, I must say, were not my own opinions, but those I judged to be about me. For myself, I didn't know what to think. There was so much of evil about the ship, it was impossible to weigh it up and portion it out: some was always left over . . .

"He's done it," Mister Pobjoy had said, neither doubting nor surprised. And Mister Pobjoy was a man I'd never known be wrong. But even so, it was hard to believe. . . . He was still too unsteady on his feet to've made the descent into the hold. It was not possible—Yet what if he'd told Mister Morris to do it? Mister Morris who'd have obeyed him to the gates of Hell? "Kill that fellow that screams so, Morris. Stick a marlin-spike in his back for me, will ye? There's a good fellow, Morris!"

When he came on deck for the burial he was cold and grave and distant, and I felt that murder or salvation were no more to him than the winking of his mind's eye.

One of the larboard cannons had been shifted and Mister Taplow's body lay on a board poked through the port, ready to be shipped into the dark sea. Mister Pobjoy had weighted him down with some heavy pots not needed in the galley so's he might rest in peace at the sea's bottom.

Every man was on deck, for it was an occasion out of the ordinary—this ceremonious laying to rest. (Much was made of this, after; and many causes propounded.)

Tapping his way carefully, with Mister Morris by his side, the Captain came to the corpse. He put his stick before him and laid both hands upon it; then with pursed lips and screwed up eyes, he spoke of Mister Taplow's chances of Heaven. They weren't very strong. "No matter," said he, "the blackest soul might mount there, and, if he repented before he died, be taken in. Even such an one as this!"

He looked up, and he looked down, as if measuring the distance. I thought he smiled; but Mister Pobjoy swore his look never flickered during the whole.

"And so to the deep I consign ye —" he said, "and may the Lord have —"

Before he could finish, the deck gave a sudden heave as if the *Charming Molly* had shrugged; and Mister Taplow's body slid down the plank and into the trough of a wave. I saw him go, for the sack tore and his red hair flamed out for a second before it was doused like a light in the water.

"— Mercy on your soul!" But the Captain was too late. Mister Taplow was gone unblessed. A very ominous silence followed this stroke of ill-luck. Then, of a sudden, came the Dutchman's voice from aloft:

"Der sail! Der sail again! Very low in der wasser! Der sail!"

The *Esperance*! Still with us in the iron wind! Mister Trumpet looked up from Taplow's grave with a quick, incredulous smile; and the spirit of the ship lightened, too; for the sight of another vessel made us feel less lonely . . . But it didn't last long. The weather worsened even as we stood there and soon the Dutchman cried down:

"Nein! Nothink! Nil!"

As we fled on before the vast wind, I thought of the queerly appearing *Esperance*—if indeed it had been she—and that very soon, perhaps already, she'd be over Mister Taplow's grave and for a while he'd be closer than he'd ever been to what he'd died for.

On the night of the fifth day after he was buried, and when

the tempest had veered to drive us a point further south, Taplow came back. Afterward it was said there were strange sights in the sky that day before the light went: horned beasts, clutching hands, and a ship in full sail.

Then the Dutchman saw the *Esperance* again for a few minutes after noon. She was lower in the water than ever, and her foretopyard seemed to be adrift. Yet somehow she seemed to be keeping with us as if her destiny was to be the same as ours, whatever our endless, south-westerly course might bring us to. Afterward, the real *Esperance* was remembered too, as well as the one in the sky: for she always seemed to appear before an unlucky happening.

It was Mister Jarvis who saw him, soon after midnight, moving along the larboard rail. He appeared with the moon as it flew out of the disturbed clouds. He was still in his faded red and white shirt which he'd worn till the day he died. And after. And there was the hole in his back, between his shoulders, where the marlin-spike had gone.

"It was him, I tell you! It was him!"

I'd never seen a man so frightened as Jarvis was on that night. I thought he would have died of it. His eyes were starting and his pocky face was all a'twitch. As the forecastle lantern swung, he kept staring into the shadows as if Taplow was hid in them. Sam Fox, in his corner, sat bolt upright; and he wasn't looking happy, either, to hear that his terrible friend was come back aboard.

"Did you see his face, old fellow? Did he turn to you?" asked Mister Trumpet.

"His face?" cried Mister Jarvis, rubbing his eyes as if to rub out the memory—"His face! It was all drenched and grey looking! Sea-water pouring down like his great head was filled with it!"

"Did he speak to you? Did he say anything?"

"Not a word. Just passed on along the larboard rail as if to show me the black hole in his back. Water coming out like his whole body was filled from the bottom of the sea."

"You've lost your wits, Jarvis!" said Mister Morris, curtly. "Taplow's dead and under the sea. He'll not be back till Judgement. You must have seen Tomkyn on the larboard watch."

But if Mister Jarvis *had* seen Mister Tomkyn, he was the last one who ever did. Mister Tomkyn was gone—vanished off the face of the ship.

"Fell overboard," concluded Mister Morris.

"Aye," concurred Mister Pobjoy. "Fell overboard—or was took!"

That night I asked him directly if he thought Taplow had indeed come back.

"Maybe, dear boy, maybe he has. And if he has, he's done this wessel a wast deal of good. He's took pore Tomkyn, rot him! And never was a soul less missed than Mister Tomkyn!" He lifted his mug of gin: "So here's to Mister Taplow, wherever he may be! May his pore nibbled bones keep warm these wet and windy nights!"

I got no more out of him than that. When he'd finished his drink, he went straight off to sleep and left me to think of Taplow in the heaving, moaning dark by myself. In all my life I'd never seen a ghost. But I'd never seen China, neither, nor the King, nor Lord Sheringham who'd had five and twenty murdering footpads hanged last year . . . I began to prickle and sweat in horrible expectation. Mister Taplow'd not cared for me much when he'd been alive: a week at the bottom of the sea wasn't likely to've changed his opinion.

If Mister Taplow was back, it was me he wanted—Mister Morris, the Captain and me! And every second I expected him!

But he came neither to the galley nor any other part of the *Charming Molly* that night—nor the next two nights till it seemed he was gone and we were haunted no more.

Then William Hughes, who was on forecastle watch, saw him and screamed, "Taplow!" But Taplow moved steady along the larboard rail, showing the great black hole in his back and never turned to answer his name.

And William Hughes clean forgot Carfax, who was on the larboard watch and came flying in and left him. It was nearly daylight when Mister Carfax was remembered and they began to search and call and shout for him. But he was gone, just as Mister Tomkyn was gone before him; and all the frantic "Carfax! Carfax! Where are ye, Carfax!" was whirled away into the black cloud behind us.

Lighter now by another man, we flew on to the south-west with a panic aboard that was spreading like the plague. Half-way to noon, a man slipped in the shrouds and was only saved by being nearly hanged. When he was taken down, he swore he'd felt a hand grasp at his ankle and jerk him loose.

"I felt his breath on me face! Taplow's breath—foul—felt it on me cheek!"

And there was no reasoning him out of it—not even by Mister Morris. For this was a man nimble as a monkey, who'd never slipped in all his years aboard. Up to topgallantyards he'd been, in gales and storms; and never tripped nor stumbled nor put a naked foot wrong. He'd been plucked from his foot-hold by a hand he'd never seen: and something had breathed in his strangling face.

The ship was sick, and even Mister Morris could not cure it: the men were more afraid of dead Mister Taplow than living Mister Morris.

All save Mister Pobjoy, who remembered coolly that: "Mister Tomkyn and Mister Carfax was a pair of shocking drunken pigs. Shed no tears for them, dear boy! They're out of their misery for good; while you and Pobjoy—if the gin holds out—pray to go on suffering in this wicked world for years and years and years!"

But Mister Tomkyn and Mister Carfax could not be so easily forgot. While in their lives nobody had cared whether they came or went, now they were dead they came by friends. Subtle Mister Trumpet was very fond of recalling what a fine fellow Mister Tomkyn had been, and remembering how he'd liked the twinkle in Mister Carfax's bleary eye. And this set on the others until the loss of Tomkyn and Carfax became a sinister warning of Mister Taplow's that he'd be revenged.

So the dead unquiet thing became a stake, a counter, between the forecastle and the poop. It became a poison that Mister Trumpet whispered into the air—and was readily breathed in . . . If a man be wronged to death, why should he not return?

Then, as he'd done with Mister Taplow himself, he began to oppose what he'd first begun. And with the same effect. Strengthening. At last, well satisfied with his achievement, he begged them, almost mockingly, to be patient awhile, to forget the Captain's wrong upon Taplow—or at least to await that dead man's pleasure in sending them another, more unanswerable sign.

So what had the marlin spike and the burying sea done to Taplow that he still walked among us? Taplow, twenty times more terrible than ever he'd been alive . . . plotting, not with one man in the hold, but stalking in every brain aboard. Twenty deadly Taplows, invisible save in turning eyes . . . Taplow in the forecastle, Taplow in the shrouds, Taplow in the sails, Taplow in the storm itself . . .

Upon the next morning, which was the beginning of the fifth week of the great storm, the wind died. We lay like a dead ship upon a dead sea. Behind us, the cloud was gone up and hung like a great black tiger in the sky. I stared at it uneasily. Was this Taplow's sign?

Chapter Nine

IF Hell is as hot as that terrible morning, then I'm not going there! The sky beat down and scorched the deck till the cannons hissed when they were spat on. And the sea! the flat, blinding, pewter-coloured sea, all a-prickle with ten thousand bits of the aching sun! there was no looking at it for more than seconds to see where we were come to—and where we were bound.

There was no talk of Taplow that day: there was no talk of anything save something to drink. Frantic Mister Pobjoy, half drowned in his own sweat, groaned to see the barrels die. Up and down the galley he slopped, and his soaking feet left pools behind them—save when he went outside and little wisps of steam came up where he'd been, as the sun dried up the wet.

By noon, it was hotter still and I thought we'd come to the end of the world. Even Mister Morris was gone inside, and the *Charming Molly* lay with naked decks under the murderous sun.

"For pity's sake go down and never come up no more!"

And when that sun was gone over and by the jib, Mister Pobjoy went out and cursed it, spitting at the misty yellow globe that glared through the canvas of the foresail. He shook his fists at it in a fury.

"Down ye go, great fry-ball! Rot and drown! Never come up no more to fry pore souls before their time!"

William Hughes, who was to take forecastle watch, shook his head uneasily. "Would you have us all in the dark, man?"

But Mister Pobjoy was gone in and never heard him. So I followed—and William Hughes went up on the forecastle head.

"William Hughes, man! Are you there?"

"Aye, Jarvis, I'm here. And it's a heavy, damp unbreathing kind of night. I'm here, Jarvis, but I wish I was not."

This was at nine o'clock in the black.

"William Hughes! Are you there, old son?"

"Here, Mister Trumpet! Here! On the fo'castle head! Sat like a toad on a sweaty wet rock. Nothing to be seen: nothing to be heard."

How close to midnight, none could recall; save it was well before the hot wind began . . .

"William Hughes! What's doing? Is anything to be seen? It's a queer, strange night and I thought I heard something—"

"There's nothing about, Sam Fox. Nothing but the soupy black. But wait—what's that down there? No, nothing. Eyes play queer tricks . . . Goodnight, Sam Fox—though it's not a good night at all and I never hope to see its like again."

Then it was—or close after—that the strange hot wind began to blow, filling the sails with sighs and groans and shifting us uneasily through the dark. Maybe there was five minutes of shouting outside before I heard them clear.

"William Hughes! William Hughes! Answer, man! William Hughes, where are you?"

William Hughes was gone.

I rushed out onto the deck and the hot wind struck me in the face like a blast from Aldgate forge. I met Mister Pobjoy whose panicky eyes flickered down on me.

"There's Hell to pay, Jack—and all the wessel's in fee!"

He blundered past into the galley, squealing and grunting like a frightened pig. "Lord have mercy on Pobjoy!"

Taplow's sign had come!

While we'd lain becalmed, the black cloud had crept atop of us! We were caught. Huge drops of rain had begun to slop down and faint lightnings flickered across the masts, turning the sails to bellying ghosts.

And all the crew, like leaves swept up by the wind, were whirled to the forecastle in a union made murderous by terror. The dead man's voice shrieked in the wind: the dead man's eyes blazed in the lightning: and the dead man's rage roared in the thunder:

"Avenge me or be blown to Kingdom Come! Kill the Captain!"

I'd a desperate thought to warn him—but was too late.

Already fork after fork of lightning was stabbing into the heart of the cloud so it began to writhe like a living thing, while the sea mounted to meet it. At last we were fallen into the black heart of the storm we'd so dreaded from the very first!

This was the end: the end of the *Charming Molly* and the murderers who sailed her: of Mister Clark and Sam Fox and their greedy hates, of Mister Pobjoy and his gin-madness, of Mister Morris and Mister Solomon Trumpet, of the strange Captain himself: and the end of Jack Holborn who'd come aboard in high spirits, had them dashed, then lifted to the skies, only to fall to the bottom of the invisible rising sea.

Down plunged the masts and up reared the deck till it stood like a streaming wall: then sideways and round as if it was enraged with every living thing upon it and would shake them off. Crazy *Molly*! Horrible *Molly*! Mad *Molly*! If thy back breaks, thou'll surely die!

Now the lightning began to flicker with terrific urgency back and forth and down to the mountainous sea. Drenched, savage faces I saw, glaring from shrouds that were swept down into the water, then up to the furious sky. Suckling and Jarvis clung arm to arm and to an iron ring in the mainmast.

Their mouths were wide and black with shouting, and their legs swung and kicked as the world sought to blot them out. Then they were brushed off, for the ship jumped and crackled as a bolt struck the foremast and toppled it into a smoking, tented ruin.

I lost my hold on a trunnion lashing and flew down the deck to the larboard rail. Sam Fox was there, reared up before me, scorched white by lightning. I crashed into his scrabbling feet—but he never saw me.

"Taplow!" he screamed—and flung his hands before his eyes. His feet weren't enough to hold him. I felt them twist, kick, rise up and saw his naked soles fly despairingly over the side.

Then I saw the ghost of Taplow. Down the rail it came,

faded red and white shirt flapping and its great head hid in
a rusty cloth.

"What d'you want with me, dead Taplow? Must I go with
the rest? Have pity on me! Have pity! Let me stay on the
world awhile! Even five minutes more!"

But still he came towards me; then the lightning blazed
and I saw clear as day what was Taplow's ghost! It was
Mister Pobjoy! Mad Mister Pobjoy! Wearing dead Taplow's
shirt! He must have stole it when he laid him out! (Cunning
Mister Pobjoy!) The *Charming Molly*'s murderous ghost:
thirsty masquerading Mister Pobjoy!

His little eyes flickered and flared as the deep-down Pobjoy
rose up and laid a hold of all his head.

"Jack!" he screeched, waving at me. "Don't say it's Pobjoy!
Don't say it and I'll spare ye! Keep—keep the secret, dear—"

Down we dipped and a yard from the ruined foremast
poked up out of the sea and clouted him on the head. He
howled and fell—and I tried to cling onto him.

He was slipping away and would have gone, had not
Mister Trumpet been washed across and helped me hold him.
I had him by the arm; it turned and jerked and strained to be
free as the sea kept plucking at him. The waves washed his
head from side to side and I saw the yard had broke his skull
and he was dying. But he had a frantic desire to confess himself before he went, and tried to drag me closer to him.

Tomkyn, Carfax and Hughes knocked in his ruined head
and troubled him. Then a wave came and washed him under
a curtain of green. He'd not the strength to talk and hold his
head steady. The sea rushed out of him, pasting his beard flat
up against his cheeks . . .

He'd done for them—Tomkyn, Carfax and Hughes. Three
drunken pigs. Pigs. And the gin was running short. So easy.
They'd shrieked at the sight of Taplow's shirt . . . Only a
small shove required . . .

The waves were coming very regularly now over the starboard beam—sometimes as high as the mainyard—and falling

upon us amidships so we were continually shook as if with a fever. Between the hollow crashes, there was a gasping as the sea sucked back from our keel only to rise up and fall over us again . . .

So he'd done for Taplow, too? No! No! He'd not laid a finger on that horrible man! So it *had* been the Captain? No! It had been Sam Fox! Sam Fox had stabbed him. Sam Fox—his friend. Went down to whisper . . . plan . . . help . . . Pobjoy saw . . . Fox in a mortal sweat that Taplow'd peach on him . . . stuck him in the back . . . not a sound . . .

A wave, higher than a house, came clean over the mainyard and left the rigging hanging down like a madwoman's hair. The arm I was holding, slid through my fingers and I caught it again at the wrist. When the spray cleared, I saw Mister Trumpet floundering wildly to anchor himself while he clutched on to Mister Pobjoy's stolen shirt. He shook his head at me—then ducked down under the next tremendous wave.

I thought Mister Pobjoy was dead, for his head seemed so loose on his neck, and he never shut his eyes against the sea. But he was still mumbling:

"Never have harmed ye, dear boy . . . never . . . ye're for Heaven . . . and—and I'm for a Judge more strict than—than Lord Sheringham . . . Put in a word for P-pobjoy, dear boy . . . when ye get there . . ."

Mister Trumpet flung up a hand in despair. His grip had torn loose. A little wave, reaching barely over the starboard rail, came now and eased Mister Pobjoy further into the sea. His wrist twitched in my hand. I had him by the left hand. His bad one. Once he'd sliced off the top joint of his forefinger with a pork-knife. When it healed, the stump was desperately tender. Made vile shudders run through him when it was touched. Couldn't abide it to be breathed on even . . . With all his last strength, he forced his good fingers up so's I shouldn't touch his stump. He went very quietly, just slipped away like he'd been secretly called.

"Look to starboard!"

The cry was aloft! The Dutchman was still at the crosstrees. Nearly flayed by the wild sea, he still clung there.

"Look to starboard! Starboard! Starboard!"

No more than a hundred yards off was the wildest sight in all the world! Another ship, under leaping, ragged canvas was bearing down on us!

"Starboard! Starboard!" the Dutchman screamed; but there was none left who could heed him. The *Charming Molly* was come upon her deathbed and not all the Dutchman's howling nor Mister Morris's wrenching at the helm could drag her off of it.

From the moment the *Esperance* was sighted (for it was that ominous ship that had come out of the dark like a racketing vengeance), till the frightful moment she struck, a careful man might have counted up to twenty.

The *Charming Molly* gave a pitiful little jerk as if to escape. But the huge and ragged *Esperance*, her yards and clew-fastenings gleaming with a strange phosphorescence caught off the sea, reared up against the starboard beam. Then she dipped and struck.

About four yards aft of amidships her iron-hooped prow drave into the *Charming Molly*'s beam, below the waterline. Her naked bowsprit slit away our shrouds with a rattle like musket-fire; then she rose with the rising of the sea and cracked us like an egg.

Though her foremast snapped and tumbled away in a pounding jumble of canvas and line, her great weight and the wildness of the sea drove her further. Our planks split asunder and our great mainmast itself (for the first time since it was set), was uncovered to its root. With its supports gone, it cracked and tore away from its bed in the keel.

Then the *Esperance*'s hull, ragged and rent where the *Charming Molly* had kissed her, shuddered vastly, as if with remorse at what she'd done. She began to rise and climb upward, towering blackly, shutting out all sight of the spitting sky. Loud suckings and cracklings came from beneath her—loud enough to drown the roaring of the wind and sea. The waters appeared to be boiling as she continued to rise and the life's air of our opened hold burst out. At the same instant, four or five great hammer-blows struck us from beneath the sea; and with one accord all the waters in the world rushed away from us!

Great waves scudded and thundered to be clear of us, as if we'd done some frightful thing! Troughs and crests fell one upon another in an enormous hurry, abandoning us to ruin.

This tremendous effect had been brought about by the undercurrent of the sea itself, which, moving contrary to its wild upper part, had dragged at the blundering keels till the huge confusion of the double wreck grated thunderously on submarine rocks!

We were stopped; and the sea rushed wildly by. Such currents as caught us move very strongly through underwater reefs, the unchanging tide forcing the waters through narrow apertures and tunnels till it gains a formidable force against which even the storm winds are powerless. Rage as they might, the tempest and the biting waves were done with us.

"Give over! Give over!"

Mister Trumpet's voice, like from ten thousand miles away; he must have been shouting for minutes before I heard him. I saw my foot was dug deep in his elbow and he was pinned back of the poop companionway. I shifted as much as I dared, and he crawled up delicately beside me—as if afraid of dislodging us from the rocks and back into the pounding sea.

"If the wind drops—we're saved!"

Side by side we lay, staring up at the overhanging bulk of the *Esperance*, huge as another sky, washed and washed again by the powerful sea. We were dazed and deafened by the loud cracks of the shattering ships and the enormous breathing of the storm. It seemed no sound could ever be heard above them; yet the sound we both did hear was tiny and faint.

It was a scrabbling on the woodwork behind us: a frantic kind of scratching.

Through a streaming window in the poop, I saw the Captain! His face, blurred and white, was pressed up against the glass.

The entire poop had been sealed off from the worst excesses of the storm and wreck, and he'd survived it all. Behind him, in the angle of the floor and wall, lay Mister Morris—alive also, though injured: his hands were clasped to his chest.

Mister Trumpet got the door open: a giant effort.

"Lucky I heard you . . . lucky I heard . . . You're all right now . . . you're saved . . . thank God I heard . . . saved you . . ."

"Saved?" panted the Captain, indignantly. "Come in out of the wet yourselves! Been trying to get the both of ye to safety since ye fell! *We* saved, indeed!"

So there were four of us left to see out that night, which was the forty-first of the storm-cloud's pursuit of us. What became of the others, I don't know. Those I saw perish, I've told of: I think the rest were in the shrouds and close below the Dutchman. They must have gone when the mainmast tore away. Maybe some of them floated to an island or were picked up by a passing vessel? Most likely not. The sea that night was too hungry to neglect even those wicked morsels. I think they are all with Taplow now. And God—in truth—knows where *he* may be.

We lay without talking, huddled against the injured Mister Morris. He'd been badly bruised when the helm had splintered away in his grasp and the Captain had dragged him to safety. Now he grunted a little with pain, but beyond that seemed well and peaceful enough. So we breathed deep and thankful and watched, through the ever washed ports, for some diminishing in the fury of the night.

It came with the dawn. Little by little the wind sank and the great sea with it.

Then the sun rose up into a clean sky and showed us a most marvellous thing. Eastward, through the windowage disaster had made in the *Esperance*, we saw the extent of the reef on which we'd foundered.

It rose out of the sea in a curving spine which merged into the hazy splendour of a beach—we were no more than a hundred yards from a shore!

The powerful sun was too bright to make out more than a scoop of white sand skirted by tall trees. But it was enough!

When we were sufficiently recovered, we prepared to leave the cabin of the *Charming Molly*, taking with us, on Mister Morris's advice, such necessities as had survived the storm.

Chapter Ten

MISTER TRUMPET's dream, so lately become nightmare— the *Esperance*—hung huge and black above us. Her hull was crusted with shellfish from the furthest seas of the earth. Mister Morris, careful, cleanly sailor that he was, eyed it with disapprobation.

She was held off us by several black teeth of rock that snouted up and bit into her timbers: which grunted warningly, being near collapse.

There was nothing living aboard her. That was plain the instant our feet slopped hollowly on her deck. She was a dead ship: glaringly dead under the pitiless sun. Even though we searched her, we knew it was useless. Nothing of life remained. What had become of her crew, only Mister Trumpet could conjecture. He said there'd been a longboat on deck. Maybe all that was left of the crew had piled into it for some reason of storm damage and gone adrift in the ocean . . .?

"Trust themselves to an open boat in such weather? Mad!"

"All right, all right!" muttered Mister Trumpet.

"What does it matter now? They're gone and we're alive. There's an end of it! But I think they went in the longboat. I knew them, I tell you . . . three especially . . . and I think they took the White Lady with them! And now she's lost for ever! Damnation take them!"

We were leaving the galley, which had been stripped bare, when Mister Trumpet let slip his odd remark. The White Lady. An abbess? A nun? What kind of crew had sailed the *Esperance* that they should take such a one aboard? And then to take so venerable a dame in the longboat with them! I puzzled stupendously to imagine the circumstance that must have led to her being aboard. And my opinion of Mister Trumpet went up, for he was honestly and honourably anxious on account of the White Lady. He was plainly distressed for her.

"There's not much time left," said Mister Morris. "The tide's rising and soon the rocks will be covered. We must be gone."

But Mister Trumpet was already gone: he was gone to the poop which we'd searched once and found no more than soiled linen, a pair of torn breeches, and a loaded pistol that Mister Trumpet swore was his, remembering certain scratches on the barrel . . .

"We'll leave him," said Mister Morris, grimly. "Let him follow if he can. He's out of his mind. A contagious sickness, from all accounts . . ."

Nevertheless, Mister Morris didn't seem to hurry unduly. Mister Trumpet had scuttled down a hatchway. We could hear him scrambling and banging about inside. Then we heard him cry out—and before we could reach him, there came the roar of a shot!

The ship quivered dangerously with it and Mister Morris

cried out: "He's done for himself! I said he was mad!"

We found him in a cabin, leaning—smoking pistol in hand—against a bulwark. His face held a look of extraordinary peace and joy! He'd shot the lock off a bound chest he'd dragged from under the bunk.

"D'you know what's in it?" he whispered, more to the gunpowdery air than to us. "D'you know? Ten million pounds! Ten millions! They left it behind. Why? Why? What became of them? The fools! To've cast off without it!"

He lifted the lid and all the wealth in the world winked its wicked eyes at us.

Mostly it was in pearls and diamonds, with handsome gold settings, but there were rubies and emeralds, too—and maybe some bits of coloured glass . . . For who could say, in so large and splendid company, that all was what it pretended to be? Nonetheless, there must have been enough in the chest to've ransomed a dozen kings: if one'd a mind to spend it so.

"Gentlemen," said Mister Trumpet, on his knees for the first time: "Now we are all become rich. Is it not stupendous?" he went on, digging among the stones with strong fingers. "Not a minute ago we were poor. Of no consequence in the world. Now we are mighty. And all in a minute!

"You, Morris, can buy and fit your own ship for trade or travel: as you will. Never a care save the wind. You, Jack, can have horses and servants—a mansion, and maybe a coat-of-arms.

"Money's made honest men of you. Money! A minute ago you were penniless pirates, scarce worth the rope they'd hang you with. Now you're men of substance that none would look sideways at.

"Even you—even—hm! you—(he looked at his unforgotten enemy, the Captain) must be a deal richer than before! Though the Devil knows what you'll do with it! Purchase, maybe, a thicker bandage for that Blind Lady you so treacherously serve?"

"Ye're a fool, Trumpet!" retorted the Captain, suddenly red—as if Mister Trumpet got under his skin too easily with his strange remark—"Even supposing all this was legally ours . . . wouldn't ye change it all for good meat and bread? What's to be done with it here in this forsaken spot?"

"Let's be out and away," grunted Mister Morris, unmoved, I thought, by his sudden improvement. "Let's be gone before the tide takes us off."

"Divide the jewels first. We must divide them," said Mister Trumpet, looking up at each of us demandingly.

"To Hell with them!"

"What d'you say, Jack?"

I looked, and dreamed of what I could buy—if ever I got back again.

"I'll take all I can carry, Mister Trumpet."

"Good lad!" said he, greatly relieved. "For we'll never manage the chest across the reef. We must take what we can carry, eh? So take what you will, gentlemen! Let no man say I was the one to stop—ah!" He gave a sudden cry. "It's here! It's here! Oh! Lord above—it's still here! Look! Look on this! Trumpet's dream! The White Lady!"

Deep in the chest he'd unearthed a huge and glittering diamond so extraordinary in its brilliance that all the cabin seemed aglow with it. It was not set, but lay like a burning egg in Mister Trumpet's trembling palm. He bent his head over it till he must have been nearly blinded by its light. This was the White Lady.

"Take what you will—save this! My darling White Lady!"

"Leave it behind!" said Mister Morris, curtly. "I've heard of that stone. It's unlucky. Accursed."

"Superstitious fool!"

"Say what you will: I'll not take a chance on fate."

"*You'll* not take a chance? *You* indeed! She's mine! I was the one who sailed this ship and dreamed of her! I was the one who—"

"—Who mutinied to thieve her?" finished the Captain. Mister Trumpet turned on him furiously; was about to say something—then thought better of it.

"Jack," he said, "take your pick of the jewels. Diamonds are richest, then rubies. Leave those with the heavy settings for they'll not be worth the carrying. Stuff 'em in your pockets, lad—but not too tight or they'll chafe as you walk."

I knelt beside him and began to pick at rings and brooches, when he chuckled and shook his head.

"Here: let me help you."

Very quickly, he began sorting out a glittering pile for me, staring sharply into the depths of each jewel as he held it to the light. Less than a second sufficed for each one: for Mister Trumpet was plainly expert. Colour seemed to guide him more than size; and weight he judged, too. Those with a bluish fire, he grunted over and put in my pile: others, he tossed aside. A lovely green stone I'd have had, he shook his head over, pointing out a flaw that, search as I might, I couldn't see.

"That's enough to set you up well," said he, and helped me tie my treasure in a square of linen ripped from the bunk. For I'd but one breeches pocket, and that rotted away by the corrosive sea.

For a while, Mister Morris and the Captain stood back; but then they, too, saw the folly of setting their faces against good fortune.

Mister Morris seemed to choose at random, as if it was more to humour Mister Trumpet and me than to please himself but the Captain was more careful.

A fine string of pearls, he took, and more coloured stones than diamonds, which he left to Mister Trumpet and me.

"You could do better, you know," said Mister Trumpet, who'd been watching him shrewdly as he chose.

"And so could you have done, once!" returned the Captain. "With your fine eye and excellent judgement—you *should* have done better—"

"My 'excellent judgement' was overruled! Overruled by— oh! beg pardon! Beg pardon! Take it then—"

He'd begun to say something else, when their questing

hands met on a diamond and ruby pendant. At once, they both let it fall, and, I noted, fine as it was, that pendant was never taken up again by either of them. It was left behind in the cabin of the *Esperance*, together with maybe a million pounds or more in trinkets too heavy for the four of us to carry away.

The way across the reef was not so plain as before. The tide had risen while we'd been in the cabin, and now there were gaps between the rocks. What had at first seemed a hundred yards, was now more like three times that distance, and sharp and treacherous into the bargain.

The closer to shore we got, the more the rocks were bedabbled with blood-red anemones, which were hideous to tread on, and stained us till it looked like our feet were torn to bloody ribbons. Once the Captain slipped on a clump of such things and nearly fell.

"Bad judgement, eh? And maybe not for the first time!" Mister Trumpet laughed delightedly, as if he'd said something witty: but the Captain was too intent to answer.

At last, we were able to step off the rocks and stand in water that reached below our knees. We had escaped from the sea. Together we turned and looked back at the double wreck. Even as we watched, the sea which had subtly crept up toppled the *Esperance* slowly on its side and it fell, with a splintering grinding sigh, on all that remained of the *Charming Molly*.

This, then, was the final end of her; under a hot sun upon a calm sea. The *Esperance* survived only minutes longer. She floated away from the reef, filled quickly with water and sank as if glad of it.

Slowly we dragged our aching feet from the sea and gazed on the land we'd come to. None of us spoke for there was an enormous silence about the wide, white bay which seemed to be enjoined on us likewise.

A sun, ten times bolder and fiercer than any I'd ever seen, stood directly over the forest, so even yet it was impossible to guess at its scope. The tufted tops of the trees were wrapped in shifting hazes and the whole dark sweep seemed to be quietly breathing . . . Maybe it stretched for five miles: maybe for five hundred. There was no present means of knowing. All we could do was to trudge across the scorching sand toward the blessed relief of its shade. When it came, it fell on us with a sudden chill, making us to shiver . . .

Mister Morris alone remained in the heat, taking sight after sight through his sextant and marking figures in the sand with the Captain's gold-topped cane.

"What God-forsaken isle is this?" called out Mister Trumpet. "Where are we, Mister Sailing-master? How far from London and which the way back?"

Mister Morris continued with his observations.

"If we set a course south-east," said he, to the Captain, "we should reach the peak of a promontory about twelve miles from here."

"Mad!" interrupted Mister Trumpet coolly. "Mad. Why go through the forest when all we've to do is go round the shore till we come to a port? I vote for going by the shore. What d'you say, Jack? Remember, old son, here on unknown land we're all equal."

"Leave the lad alone, Trumpet. Don't force choices on him. What can he know of this land—or of you and me?"

"Oh! beg pardon! Didn't know he was a—a ward of the Court!"

"Go by the shore and you'll fry in the sun," said Mister Morris wearily. "And I, for one, wouldn't stop you. But you'll leave the boy. Come, man, be sensible! Here we've come to what's most likely the West coast of Africa—"

"—Or the Western coast of the Indies, or the Western coast of China!" jeered Mister Trumpet.

"And our best plan," went on Mister Morris, as if Mister Trumpet hadn't spoken, "is to make for high ground for a vantage, for a scope of the country—a sweep of the coast. Better twenty miles with a prospect at the end of them than maybe two hundred for nothing. Maybe a river takes its source up there—" He pointed high to the south-east, "and we can follow it down to the sea. For if there's to be a port of any size, there's no more likely place than that."

Twenty miles. The silence fell on us again as we stared into the blackness in whose outermost shade we lay. How long would it take us? How many miles could we reckon to the day? Or how many days to the mile? The ground was close covered with twisting roots, thick as a strong man's legs. Also there was mud to be seen: mud which warned of swamp. These things were visible. What lay beyond?

Mister Trumpet frowned uneasily and fingered his fortune. Come what may, he was wedded to the White Lady till death did them part. Mister Morris had turned his back on the forest and was staring, as if for the last time, upon the sea which was his right and proper home.

"I hold you responsible, Mister Morris!" exclaimed Mister Trumpet, at length. "I call upon all of you, here and now, to remember I was against the forest. Before it's too late—think again! Twenty miles through *that*! Who knows what murderous beasts lurk in there? See! There's swamp as well! D'you know what that means? Fever! In what case are we to fight fever? And snakes! All right! Supposing we escape the fever and reptiles . . . what then? What of the savages that haunt these parts? For the last time, I beg you, abandon the forest. Go by the shore!"

"Morris," said the Captain, after a pause in which Mister Trumpet's words were considered. "Ye've heard what the good fellow says. Does it shake ye?"

"No. Of course there are dangers in the forest! Maybe as he says—great dangers. I've not shut my eyes to them. But there's death along the shore. Certain death. We'd not survive above five hours. Under such a sun I've seen men scorched to the blackened bone."

So the forest it was to be: the dark and dangerous forest. That was the way for four rich men.

Chapter Eleven

FOR fifteen days we toiled, and bled, and wept, and raged towards Mister Morris's promontory: during which time we suffered two terrible losses, and much else besides . . . We travelled by day, which was no more than a tremendous green twilight: then, when the seasonal rains fell down like grapeshot on the forest's lofty roof, we slept among the roots. Sometimes, leaves, overburdened with water, would uncup, and a cataract would drop like a silver plummet through the green-black air. These, when we caught them, served us for drink: for the water of the swamp was poisonous. Beyond the swamp, the forest's floor was all tumbled with soft leaves, very pleasant-seeming to sleep upon: but that we never did. Once when I was—but that I must tell in its proper order, on account of what it led to . . .

We began our journey close on noon, when the shadows had shrunk and the sea-water dried on us, leaving patches of white salt on our faces and arms like we were afflicted with a sea-leprosy.

Our course was plotted and a likely opening found. This, after we'd dined off some green, wood-tasting fruits that Mister Morris knew as "Mariners' Saviours". "Perishers", Mister Trumpet thought would have been a better name for them, for the griping pains they gave him would be the death of him, he said. Close upon noon, then, of that day, we looked our last on sun, sea and sky—and entered into the great forest.

Mister Morris led the way, very delicately—for the horrible peril of swamp began where the sun left off: grey-brown and thickly steamy, all lecherous with roots and patches of solid-seeming ground that groaned and blubbered to the lightest touch. Neither land nor sea was this part of the forest, but a kind of half-idea in the world's mind.

For about an hour we continued along a thin, firm path across the bog: a path that, somehow or another, seemed to've been marked out for us. If the path appeared to divide, there were always broken sticks and twigs about the safer way. It was as though we were following in the footsteps of some sure-footed creature . . .

Presently, the way grew wilder and the dense mud thinner and more watery, till, at times, it was like a warm stinking lake. Hereabouts were dagger-beaked birds of bright plumage, haunting the ragged bushes: for there were fishes in this part of the swamp—and flies, fever-flies, making a shivering net . . .

Mister Morris came to a halt. The firm ground had dwindled. To the left lay a yard of evil-looking bog, then a patch of reeded green: maybe safe—maybe not. To the right lay a slowly stirring log, not rotten; nor yet secure. This log was wedged into the mud four yards off. Directly ahead lay nothing but steaming ruin. Or we could have turned back.

Mister Morris was for going by the log. Mister Trumpet was for leaping the easy yard to the clump of green. I was for either: so long as I wasn't the first to try. The Captain poked at the log with his stick and said:

"Ye must have reasons, Morris: ye're a reasonable man. Come, out with them."

"What reasons!" put in Mister Trumpet, angrily. "What more can he have than any of us? Like us, he must go by the look of things. And why should his look be better than mine? Eh? Sharper eyes? The Devil he has! He's no more knowledge than Jack, here, of swamp and bog! I've seen them before. In Virginia. (In Virginia, your lordship, if you please!) That log will twist off the mud and we'll flounder and sink. The mud is quick, not solid. The patch on the left is for safety. Look! There's more beyond."

"Morris, yer reasons, man," pursued the Captain.

Mister Morris scowled and rubbed his sore chest.

"The log seems *put* there—" He paused as if understanding

77

that his reasons weren't reasons, but something deeper that he trusted more; and so would have us trust likewise. But out of respect to the Captain, he went on: "It's driven into the mud— not resting easy. I take it as a sign. All the way we've come, we've been guided by such signs. Broken branches, flattened reeds and the like. At each division of ways, we've taken what seemed to've been marked out. And we've come safe. This log— to me—seems marked out. Therefore, I trust it."

All this while, Mister Trumpet must have been debating in his own mind whether his or Mister Morris's view was the wiser. As the Captain nodded, he came to his conclusions.

"Out of my way!" he shouted suddenly, and made the yard-wide leap to the patch of green. "I'll show you which way's right!"

The Captain moved quick—astonishingly quick: but whether he meant to prevent the disaster or bring it about, was impossible to say. Maybe Mister Trumpet's foot tangled in the stick as it was raised? Maybe the stick *was* held up to stop him? Maybe a foot slipped in the mud? Maybe a foot was *put* in the mud? Ten thousand maybe's won't find the answer now.

In the same instant he was standing among us, so it seemed, Mister Trumpet was suddenly chest-high in the swamp!

Many a time in the streets of Holborn I've sniggered to see a glorious gentleman slip and squelch into the kennel-mud: but never no more. I'll not laugh again. For I'll always remember this other mud and Mister Trumpet, shrieking and failing as his poor arms beat the oozy slime into a slow, black boil. The reeded patch had given way.

Sometimes he was clear to the waist, and the swamp was thrown across his back like a rolled robe: sometimes I dreaded he was gone . . . till his patched white face turned up and something akin to a hand grew at us out of the bog. Once I saw the slow dance of his legs as he seemed to caper free in a shiny pit. Then the sides sank in and all the blind life in the marsh must have snuggled him.

Mister Morris, being half-way across the log, and in great danger himself, could do nothing. He could only watch in startled pity. Great as was his dislike of Mister Trumpet, he could not but be moved by his horrible situation.

So it was to the Captain and me—his two worst enemies— to do what we could by leaning and reaching to snatch at his slippery hand. As I caught it, I remembered, of a sudden, that other hand I'd held—and let go in the storm: luckless Mister Pobjoy's . . .

"Not so hard!" panted the Captain. "Gently . . . gently . . . little at a time . . ."

"Easy . . . easy . . ." muttered Mister Morris, as if a shout would have startled us into letting go.

Little by little, now, he came towards us; for the forces of the swamp that held him yielded better to persuasion than to frantic heaving. At last, he came alongside the log, and, on its safe, far side we gouged him out—huge with slime.

He could neither walk nor stand as he was, being too heavy; so we scraped him clean as we could with sticks and leaves, removing upwards of a dozen leeches from his naked flesh. Afterwards, he was able to help himself, when we came to a pool of clean water . . .

But before this, even when the slime was thickest on him and he still wore his leeches like buttons, he fished and fumbled for his jewels. The White Lady was still with him, though Death the pair of them had nearly parted.

"Ye'd have died for it," said the Captain. "And very nearly did."

"And you'd have killed for it!" returned Mister Trumpet, his mouth making a sudden flower in his crusted face. "And very nearly did!"

Although this was plainly untrue—for if Mister Trumpet had sunk in the swamp, the stone would have gone with him— and the remark of a man too shaken to consider, the Captain said nothing, and left Mister Trumpet's accusation like a breeding maggot in the air.

After this, Mister Trumpet conducted himself very easily; especially for one who believed himself to've been nearly murdered. Perhaps he judged himself more safe now the attempt had been made and failed?

To me, who'd seen as much as anyone, it was very strange. For, though it was possible the Captain had indeed pushed, or tripped Mister Trumpet as he'd leaped, there was no doubt he'd done much to save him: even to straining his old wound till it bled again slightly.

By next day, thank God, we were across the swamp and upon firm ground. But otherwise, there was little enough to be thankful for. Sometimes, even now, when I'm alone at night in a tall, narrow street and boards creak and unseen folk stir in the darkened houses, I fancy myself back in that huge, brooding gloom, walking . . . walking . . . walking . . . And Mister Trumpet—

"Who's there? What's that? It moved! Look! Look!"

"Quiet, man!" flung Mister Morris—for he'd no foreknowledge of what was amiss. He was busy with his compass, plotting us east by south-east.

"You're mad, Morris! Mad!" Mister Trumpet ranted on: "We should have gone by the shore! What a dance you're leading us now! A Morris-dance, eh? He—he!"

Then, by late afternoon, it became plain that all wasn't well with Mister Trumpet. From complaining of the patient little master who'd become the especial enemy of his frantic wit, he began to complain of the cold when there was none. Terrible pains tore through his head and left him dazed and panting. Then they came again and he had to shut his eyes against the green that was blinding him. So he couldn't see all the time, and was in danger of plunging off on his own, maybe back to the swamp. For he'd borne something inside him away from the swamp—and it strove to draw him back. Mister Trumpet was infected with the swamp-fever.

Now he began to rave all the while in a high-pitched

whining voice that was a mockery of his ordinary tones. What he said made no sense to any save himself, and he'd fall silent to listen to the echoes of his own whirling words.

We could go no further. Mister Trumpet had to stop. A soft pile of leaves would have made a fine bed for him.

"Here," said I. "Lay him here."

I poked with my naked foot—and woke a sleeping snake! Foul, frightened little weaving thing! Up came its flat green head—and Mister Morris shot it off!

"Are ye bit? Are ye bit?" cried the Captain and Mister Morris together, rushing to my side. No: I wasn't bit. Save thorn scratches and filth there was nothing to show on my foot. Nevertheless I was badly frightened.

But all this—I mean concerning my fright with the snake— I'd not have told save on account of what it led to. While the Captain was thanking God for the sureness of Mister Morris's aim, Mister Trumpet had been unobserved.

"Lord Sheringham!" came his high voice, suddenly. "Look! Look!"

I cannot tell how strange it was to hear the great judge's name so clear in that far-off brooding place. So plain came out "Lord Sheringham", that it might have been in his own stern Court, packed with innocence and guilt.

Why Lord Sheringham? Had delirious Mister Trumpet seen him in a shadow, wigged and nosegay'd, and ready to pass a famous judgement?

"Hang a man with this! He—he!"

The lunatic had somehow got hold of the shattered snake and was holding it up in a hangman's noose. His eyes rolled and sweat poured and dripped off his beard as he tottered towards his arch-enemy, the Captain.

"Look, Lord Sheringham! Happy memories, eh?"

Mister Morris went forward to seize him, but Mister Trumpet danced aside.

"You'll not catch me in your Morris-dance! Never no more! Oh, you'll not catch me again . . . *Though I roam ten thousand miles . . ."* He began to chant; then stopped and made a quick pass to coil his noose round the Captain's neck. The Captain warded him off—but gently. Now he made for me, and I stood back. So he put the dead snake behind him and turned his head aside as he talked, lest some efflorescence of his, or noxious miasma, caught me in its net.

"I've a fever, Jack: a deadly fever. I know it. I got it in the swamp. D'you know when? When he touched me. When Lord Sheringham laid his poisonous hand on mine. I'd a cut on that hand, so I know it. He wants to kill me, Jack, because I know who he is. But now you know. Now you know who his Blind Lady is—the Blind Lady with the scales and sword. Dame Justice. Did you think she was related to my White Lady, eh? I thought you wondered. Ha—ha! Well, in this world maybe they're sisters-in-law! In law! He—he!

"But now you all know—so he'll have to kill you all! So beware of his touch! Beware of Lord Sheringham's touch. The judge's evil!"

"He's mad."

Mister Morris spoke very quiet. "Like a dog."

"Morris! What are ye doing?"

Mister Morris was examining his pistol—which had once been Mister Trumpet's, off the *Esperance*. He was looking at it coolly, making sure the charge was competent in the second barrel. He knelt down to where Mister Trumpet had collapsed, clutching at his head. Now Mister Morris laid the barrel to Mister Trumpet's temple, gently moving away his fingers first.

"I'm going to blow out his infected brain. Like I would with a dog. Jack: turn aside."

"Morris! Stop!"

I don't know whether Mister Morris would have shot Mister Trumpet then—in the heat, or rather the coldness of the moment—and so put an end to him and what he knew, if the Captain hadn't forced the pistol aside with his stick. He took a great chance. The movement might have exploded it:

but he'd relied on the authority in his voice to draw Mister Morris's finger off the trigger.

Mister Morris looked up. He ran his hand along the pistol barrel as if the stick had marked it. He disliked wilful damage to anything.

"You must bear Lord Sheringham a close resemblance for it to haunt this fellow so."

"That I do."

"Remarkably so?"

"Remarkably."

Mister Morris got to his feet somewhat slowly. The expression on his face signified nothing beyond a certain intentness. He seemed to've forgotten the calamitous Mister Trumpet entirely.

"And much else in common besides?"

"Much else indeed."

"Even to being the same man?"

"Even to that."

The pistol had somehow come to point directly at the Captain's chest. It was quite unwavering. Mister Morris had an unusually strong wrist.

"Strange—clever, even—I never guessed—"

"Why? Why should you?"

"Because I thought I knew you."

"You were mistook."

"We've been together long—"

"So—?"

"—I'd grown to esteem you—"

"For what?"

"Being what you were."

The Captain remained perfectly still, endeavouring to stare into Mister Morris's implacable eyes. His last friend lost, he stood uncomfortably alone in the world.

"D'you mean to shoot me—for being otherwise . . . otherwise than you thought me?"

"Why—would you pray first?"

"No, sir!"

"A point in your favour, that. I'd have thought you'd knelt for the effect of it."

"If I'm to be judged, it'll not be on my last seconds."

"Then God help you if it's on the rest."

Mister Morris looked down to his pistol barrel, and then to the Captain's chest. The distance was about four feet.

"You may as well live, then," he said, in a voice that was neither contemptuous nor bitter nor even resigned. (Likewise there was neither forgiveness nor mercy in it.) Mister Morris suffered his utter shipwreck in a gentlemanly calm.

"Jack," he said to me, somewhat harshly—"so now we see there's nothing great or big in this world save a fool . . ."

So Mister Trumpet's devil was out. He lay back and seemed to be sleeping—as if the burden he'd shed had eased him. Now it was Mister Morris who was possessed by it. Yet for my part, at that time, I was no more than bewildered.

The great Lord Sheringham here at my side? The famous Lord Sheringham my companion? In honest truth I could feel no more than that! Maybe it was because of the extraordinary circumstance: of the dying Mister Trumpet, the broken snake, our wealth and passions—maybe it was because of all these turbulent things that nothing could seem head above shoulders strange.

For I had no difficulty in believing him to be Lord Sheringham. I could have believed anything of that cold, frail man with his queer fish-like eyes and now ruined country complexion. But I could not conceive of what had unseated Mister Morris. That the Captain had done many things that would have ill become Lord Sheringham, I knew. But what had the wise and honourable Lord Sheringham done that was so monstrous in the Captain? What could a good man do that would disgrace a bad one—even in the bitter eyes of his friend? Or was it that Mister Morris was so loyal a servant of evil that *all* goodness was his deadly enemy? He clutched at his chest as though his heart had received a fatal blow.

"God save you, Lord Sheringham," spoke Mister Trumpet, suddenly, in his delirium, "You are a merciful man. I thank you for my life."

Chapter Twelve

HOPE for Mister Trumpet was abandoned soon after midnight. Before that, there'd seemed a chance—seemed some purpose, so to speak, in our crouching about him, watching for a diminishing in the fury of his fever. But then the seasonal storm aggravated it. The tremendous uproar on the forest's roof plainly gave him no respite when he needed it most. When it passed, he lay, seeming to sleep, but with wide-open eyes, staring at the darkness above. So fixedly did he stare that it was impossible not to look upward from time to time to see what captured him so entirely. But there was nothing— only the very palpable dark.

This blackness, as I've said, was very palpable so that two yards in it gave a kind of concealment, as if behind a double curtain of widow's muslin: beyond that, secrecy was absolute—the great trees and all their paraphernalia of roots and lofty branches were gone like a daydream in the wakeful night. If there was a world outside of our small being, it went its ways very quiet and stealthy and never gave us cause to suspect its being.

To look down on Mister Trumpet's eyes was not pleasant, for they showed so little of life or sense. The shivering we could do nothing for, and it was very distressing to watch.

His heart grew remarkably quick and faint, and his breathing long-spaced and so shallow that it scarcely lifted his neat, round chest. Each breath now seemed like to be his last, and it became uncannily absorbing to watch for the one that would be followed by no other.

Though nothing we could say would disturb him, our talk was all soft and in whispers. Then Mister Morris moved off and signed me to follow to a place about seven or eight feet down a gently increasing slope. The distance was shrewdly chosen: for it was close enough to observe the others—though, dimly—and far enough off for Mister Trumpet, should he come to himself briefly, not to be distressed by seeing that we were digging his grave.

From time to time, whenever a faint sound of movement was heard, Mister Morris would look up to the quiet pair above us. He would look very intently, keeping motionless, with his knife maybe stuck half in the earth, till his old companion—the one-time Captain—felt the look and returned it.

What thoughts passed between them then, God knew: but they were profoundly uneasy ones. Mister Morris would fall to working again and such of his face and expression that showed was bitter and hostile.

Nothing the great judge could do altered this—not all of his solicitude for the sick man—his ceaseless tending—his efforts to ease, even to the wiping away of sweat that trickled down to Mister Trumpet's defenceless eyes, and the clearing of spittle from his bubbling mouth lest he choke with it— nothing softened the long, hard looks Mister Morris gave him.

These looks of Mister Morris's were frightening in their suddenness and quiet: for he kept mighty close counsel. They had a horrible bitterness about them as if he was understanding how the Captain, in all their days together, had pushed him— Mister Morris—one way, and stealthily gone another himself: that, while the Captain had whistled up the wind, it was Mister Morris alone who'd sailed before it on the way of damnation.

For I don't think it was any single act done by Lord Sheringham that had so turned Mister Morris against the Captain. He was ever too steady a man to be capsized by one thing. Time alone would have corroded him: time spent and mistook.

After about an hour of hard, blind work among roots and stones that clung very fierce to their anchorage, some ghosts, that had been waiting for Mister Trumpet to die, lost patience and entered his head.

Among these ghosts of Mister Trumpet's, was one in particular that distressed him: the ghost of a Virginian gentleman.

Also the White Lady was there, with this Virginian. In some way he'd got hold of it and was tantalizing Mister Trumpet.

"No! No! No!" groaned Mister Trumpet, remembering some unlucky circumstance. And then he began pleading with a man called "Evans" who'd somehow come in: Evans and some friends of his.

"For God's sake! For God's sake! Don't kill him!"

But it seemed they did. Whether or not, he, Mister Trumpet, was ever a party to the plan or only a helpless witness, was hard to say. But I think he'd always intended to steal the stone and, even in this last extreme, would not abandon it.

There must have been a panic in the room, following the murder, for Mister Trumpet began to twist and turn as if he was once more trying to escape.

"The children!" he screamed out: "Look! Look! The children! They've seen us! Oh God! We're done!"

At first I thought they were children of the murdered man come suddenly into the room. But they were otherwise; and the actual circumstance must have been uncanny and indeed frightening.

They were black children—most likely bred by the Virginian's slaves—and they had been watching through the window. These inquisitive little black ones had watched their master being strangled. Then they had seen the White Lady—

which was the cause of it all—picked up and pocketed. Then they must have fled for their lives. Witnesses . . . witnesses . . . dangerous little children . . . nimble as monkeys . . impossible to catch and kill . . .

This disaster haunted Mister Trumpet so violently that it must have been punishment enough, having suffered it once, to suffer it now, over and over again.

"A bad business," muttered Mister Morris. "That stone is unlucky. It's brought calamity wherever it's gone. It's known for it!"

"The children!" moaned Mister Trumpet. "Keep away, little children . . ."

Now Mister Morris's prophecy became fulfilled. There was quarrelling about the stone. Evans must have seized it—and Mister Trumpet groaned and fought with this other ghost to possess it. He was hugely distressed to feel it gone: this Evans was a formidable opponent—too strong, too fierce, too murderous even as a ghost.

So Lord Sheringham took the great diamond out of the jewel-bag and held it up to Mister Trumpet—to set him at rest.

And indeed, it had some effect on him. The stone, somehow catching what faint light there was—from the phosphorescent moss that always glowed most after the rain—concentrated this light and reflected it with remarkable brilliance, almost as if it carried its own inner source of light. It was a peculiarity of this diamond alone, an uncommon skill in its cutting together with a singular purity of substance, that caused it to charm the light even out of a night as black as a pocket. Small wonder it was so much desired: there could never have been anything like it.

Mister Trumpet sighed and inclined himself towards it. It was almost possible to see his tormented, dripping face in its light . . . And above him crouched the dim form of the Judge, as if guarding him from more distracting ghosts. He seemed to be content.

Then—either his dream jerked back, or another circumstance of peculiar terror beset him. He gave a loud cry and began to shout in an extreme of panic:

"They're back! The children are come back! Their eyes—little black jewels! They've come for the White Lady! It's in their stony black eyes! They'll kill me! Save me—save me from the little burning children!"

He began to thresh about with the utmost violence.

"The death-agony," muttered Mister Morris, somewhat shakily. "I think it has come."

Lord Sheringham seemed to've been taken by surprise. He lost the advantage. Much too late, he flung himself forward to prevent the violent man from destroying himself.

For a few seconds the dim forms struggled together so's they took on the likeness of a single, giant insect—of countless arms and legs—contending with something deadly and invisible. Harsh cries came from it: twigs crackled under its shifting weight.

"Keep still, man! For God's sake, lie still—you'll kill yourself!" I heard Lord Sheringham cry out; and then Mister Trumpet's distracted:

"The children! The demon children!" as he battled against his helper and his dream; not knowing one from the other. And then this monstrous, beating insect seemed to divide—to split abruptly asunder as if it had wrenched itself in two. The one half jumped back and fell into the dark with a grunt of pain. The other lay still for a moment before being galvanized by a further burst of intolerable energy into several loud shrieks and jerkings off the ground.

Then the diseased man appeared to be forced upright and propelled violently and uncertainly down the slope towards us. Forces other than his own will had hold of him. All the while he came at us he was clawing the air with great industry —as if swaddled in an unseen net.

From his first appalling jerking and throwing off of Lord Sheringham to his present distracted approach, all was accomplished extraordinarily quickly.

"The children! The burning children! They've stolen away my White Lady!"

"Leave him!" whispered Mister Morris, as he came down at us. "There's nothing to be done for him. He cannot keep going so!"

Mister Morris was right. With a queer, pig-like grunt, Mister Trumpet's legs turned to rubbish and he collapsed into his own half-dug grave.

"Is he dead, now?"

Mister Morris never answered. Instead, he packed up some earth under Mister Trumpet's head and moved a stone that pressed his cheek. Then, as Lord Sheringham came stumbling out of the dark, said:

"He is sleeping now. I think maybe he will recover."

The fever must have burnt itself out. Mister Trumpet lay sleeping, drained of his horrors.

But there was something else extraordinary, too: something not quite so joyous—and indeed, sinister. The White Lady had vanished. It had gone from where Lord Sheringham had left it. And a thing like that wasn't easily overlooked.

At first we thought Mister Trumpet had snatched it up and then unluckily let it fly from his hand. So we searched every stick of the ground he'd covered. There was no trace of it. Nothing. Drops of shining water, wet pebbles, a glittering leaf . . . never more than that.

God knows how long we looked before we were left to face that other extraordinary truth: it was gone—utterly vanished, even as though the burning children of Mister Trumpet's dream had come out of the brooding dark and stolen it away.

But I think Mister Morris had some other sort of explanation—though he kept his customary close counsel. It was only in the occasional quick look he gave the searching judge that it was betrayed: and I understood he suspected there was more in Lord Sheringham's desperate struggle to preserve Mister Trumpet than had met our eyes. He believed that man—his one-time friend—had stolen the White Lady. And this belief served to drive a deeper wedge than ever between them—and indeed, between all of us.

Chapter Thirteen

WHEN the sun rose up, all the million birds of the forest began to sing: high up in the tangled green, they screeched and teemed in their invisible hosts.

We lay upon a gentle slope, which was the only gentle thing about that fierce, tremendous place with its trees whose tops we never saw, and whose living creepers swung and looped and arched to the eye's unending confusion—like festoonings left over from a giant's coronation.

Lord Sheringham and Mister Morris had gone hunting for food. They'd taken a pair of loaded pistols and left me to watch over the sleeping Mister Trumpet. They were not to be gone long. That had been agreed. The forest must be full of edible game and there was nothing else to detain them. Come what may, I was not to stir from the sick man's side. He looked as innocent as a babe as he slept in the shallow scoop that was to have been his grave. All hatred and vengeful thoughts seemed purged out of him by his fever. I wondered if they'd return when he awoke, giving him back his sharp, sometimes spiteful, look, with its quick sly smiles that slipped round his face like oil . . .

Then I began to wonder if I was truly glad he wasn't going to die, for he'd not been the most peacemaking of companions. If he'd died—as Taplow had died—leaving a piece of himself in each of our minds, then the humanity his fever had stirred in Lord Sheringham would remain as long as did the memory of Mister Trumpet. So he'd have done a better service by going out of the world on a compassionating note than if he stayed in it to sour it again. For I feared for him and us when he should awake. There'd be earthquakes in his brain when he discovered he'd lost the White Lady indeed.

Presently, under the racket of the birds, I thought I heard the hunters, tramping and crackling about and calling to one another. I hoped they'd return before Mister Trumpet awoke: I'd no wish to break the news of his loss by myself. A stray piece of sunlight caught a pistol barrel—or a button: flashed, then passed by. One of the hunters must have spared me a glance through some gap in the trees; for I felt it fall upon my back. Strange, how one can feel something as insubstantial as a look . . .

Now Mister Trumpet's eyelids were quivering under the ever-strengthening light, and I began to stare about, anxiously. I thought I heard him mutter, "White Lady . . . White Lady . . .", but when I turned back he'd gone peaceful again and brought his palms together under his cheek.

Lord Sheringham and Mister Morris had been gone above half an hour and I began to dread they were stalking, not edible game, but each other. That somewhere in the deceiving forest, Mister Morris was leaning, looking along a barrel, waiting to blast a last hole through a head he hated. And maybe Lord Sheringham, comprehending this, was also planning an "accident".

The shot, when it came, put a period to my speculations at their uneasiest. The whole living forest burst into alarmed life as if in protest against a sudden death!

Then the echoes died away and Mister Trumpet opened his eyes, smiled and said, calm as kiss-your-hand, "And how are *you*, Jack, this fine-feathered morning?" He laughed. "Ye gods, but I've been through it! Eh, old son?"

But I was still too dazed by the uproar to agree with him,

and still wondering whether Mister Morris had shot Lord Sheringham or Lord Sheringham had shot Mister Morris when they both came stumbling back together—with the carcass of a deer between them! They were flushed, much scratched; but there were smiles, too. The only blood that flowed was from the small brown deer.

"Ye're a lazy dog, Trumpet! Snoozing while we hunt! But I'm glad to see ye awake at last! Mighty glad!" Lord Sheringham laughed happily—for all the world as if Mister Trumpet had indeed only overslept himself after a late and cheerful night. "Wouldn't ye say he was a lazy dog, Morris?"

But Mister Morris wouldn't grant it aloud: he only smiled and smiled.

The world was suddenly a bright place: what with the pair of cheerful hunters, Mister Trumpet fresh out of his fever, and me, wondering how there could ever have been enmity between any of them!

What had wrought this change, I don't know: absorption in a common enterprise, most likely. The alarms of the night were forgot: also its suspicions.

Mister Morris squatted down and began to skin the dead beast with his knife. He worked quickly and cleanly, like a Smithfield man; never tearing the pelt, spilling little blood, and always knowing where to cut next. The spindle-thin legs, which I'd have thought would have been difficult, he managed as neatly as if he'd been drawing off a pair of gloves . . .

Then, while we dined off the tough, warm meat, talk between the four of us took many an agreeable turn, warming, as it were, to the invisible sun. It was Mister Trumpet—of all people—who set the pace by begging Lord Sheringham's pardon for betraying his secret: and from there we ranged far and wide, like we were four gently talkative friends met most pleasantly in the Park upon a Sunday morning.

Of all times, I remember this the most happily: for though what we talked of is mostly forgot, there was such a desire to be free and open with one another as if one's heart was a possession only made valuable by sharing . . .

I think it was Mister Morris who said we all seemed born anew—or words to that effect—and that the storm and wreck had sheared away our histories and cast us, washed and upright, upon this fierce and beautiful place. Then he broke off with a fit of coughing over his meat and it was left to Mister Trumpet to draw the next conclusion that ours was the chance to begin our lives afresh and remain henceforward pleasing in each other's eyes.

But the shadows began to gather again. Lord Sheringham, at first agreeing, began to have reservations. Willingly, he said, he'd forget any man's past—as long as that man could forget it himself. But as long as he remembered, he'd remind the world likewise.

At this, we all looked down, and Lord Sheringham—God knows why!—whispered:

"White Lady . . . White Lady . . ."

A troubled look came into Mister Trumpet's eyes, as if he was trying to remember something that eluded him.

"D'you know," he faltered, "there was a dream I had. A queer, placeless sort of dream about some black-eyed children . . ."

We, all of us, held our breath as Mister Trumpet mused. "It's nearly all gone from me now: and yet it troubles me like a tooth that's going to ache."

Now although we knew that, sooner or later, he'd discover his loss, it was terrible to watch him stumbling nearer and nearer the moment of discovering. Already looks flickered over his face that were cousins to the quick, sharp ones I'd hoped were gone forever. His eyes kept fading between memory, dream and suspicion . . .

"They wanted it, y'know . . . badly. I could see it . . . it comes back . . . it comes back . . ."

He rubbed his earthy hand across his forehead, leaving three fierce lines over his eye and down his cheek. "So real

. . . so very real . . . I could almost . . ." He reached for
his jewel-bag. "I—I must have a look . . . It's a—a madness
with me. I know—but I must look—"

He began to scowl in a frightened sort of way as he fumbled
in the jewel-bag, and then in his shirt and breeches. Even as
I stared, his face seemed to shrink and pale and the three black
marks across it grew livid, like the marks of a lash. He scratched
half-heartedly in the torn earth, then stopped and looked up
at each of us. To do him justice, he managed a sort of laugh.

"W—which of you did it, eh? A—a joke! Ha! ha! I—I've taken
it well, haven't I? A joke! Well—give it up, now—friends!"

He turned to me, to Mister Morris, to Lord Sheringham,
supplicatingly—though still attempting to smile. He tried to
read our eyes, watched our lips, to see if we answered his
smile: looked for a twitch, a sparkle that would betray we
were pretending, carrying on the great joke.

But there was nothing: only pity. He could not believe it.
He began to search himself again, and the ground about him—
looking up quickly with eyes that were at once desperate and
accusing. Where now was his dream, and Mister Morris's
dream, of being born anew?

"Trumpet, man," began Mister Morris; but Mister Trumpet
turned on him in a fury as if Mister Morris had come between
him and his accursed jewel.

"D'you think one of us has stole it?" flung Mister Morris.
He gave a quick look to Lord Sheringham as he spoke. "Your
stone is—lost!"

"Lost?" screamed Mister Trumpet. "What d'you mean,
lost? How can it be—lost? Has it legs, hands, power of movement? Can it make its own way off? Can it *spirit* itself away?
Did it run? Which way? Into a pocket? Is *that* the way it ran?"

He was half mad, I knew, and the fever was much to blame,
being still strong in his blood at that time: but he tore down
the last frail fabric of our pleasant dream—ripped it in shreds
and flung it in our desolate faces. Mister Trumpet was Mister
Trumpet—and what he'd always been. His name was branded

on his heart, and when that leaped, pain spelled out the letters scarred there.

And Lord Sheringham was all *he'd* ever been; and Mister Morris's suspicion seemed not so wild . . .

But Mister Morris stood his ground. He, of all of us, still remembered our dream, our idea, and he was the one who tried to save it. But he could not: and I saw in his eyes that he knew he was failing, yet would not give up because there was a way, even if not exactly the one he'd chosen . . . And he understood *that*, too, I think . . .

So we began again and searched for a hundredth time, tearing aside bushes and bracken, dragging back creepers, clawing up ground: and always under the frantic, disbelieving eyes of Mister Trumpet who crouched wretchedly on the edge of his half-dug grave.

"It must be somewhere—it must be somewhere! Look! Look again! And again! Only don't give up! Not now! I'll go mad if you give up! It must, must, *must* be here! Or was it stolen by the children? The burning little children of my dream?"

Chapter Fourteen

WHEN darkness came, we gave up the search: but Mister Trumpet would not, could not, abandon it.

Lord Sheringham and Mister Morris tried to keep awake, but for how long, I don't know: for I drifted off very soon with my head against a tree-trunk and my hands between my knees. This was my first sleep in two days and I think nothing in the world would have kept me from it: yet I woke in the middle of the night. I woke to the burning look of Mister Trumpet's eyes—a foot away from my own.

Behind him, the darkling forest groaned and twinkled, like it was peering in on itself. The other two had fallen asleep close at hand. I could hear them breathing. I could not see them. I spoke in a whisper.

"Have you been awake all the while?"

"You talked in your sleep."

"What about? What did I say?"

He breathed deep: "I heard you say, 'White Lady . . . White Lady . . .'"

"I—I don't remember—"

"You were asleep. It must have been on your conscience."

"On my brain, you mean! And not surprising, after the day! Searching—searching. But I never thought I talked in my sleep. Did I look—troubled?"

"Never saw your face. I was watching—our friends!"

"Do you think—I took it, then?"

"No. But maybe you've an—idea?"

"I haven't. I saw nothing. First I knew was—" and I told him. He listened, shaking his head.

"White Lady . . . White Lady . . ."

Mister Morris was muttering in that strange voice of one who answers a dream.

"Damn him! Was it Morris? I don't believe it was Morris! He hated it!"

"Do you think it was Lord Sheringham?"

"I don't know."

"Ask him to turn out his bag."

"He—he! I've done that for him—already! It's not there."

"He's innocent, then!"

"Innocent? That man innocent?"

"Didn't you agree we'd start afresh?" I said, after a pause.

"Ah! I forgot! All fresh! All innocent! Jack—heart of gold: Morris—heart of gold: his lordship—heart of—diamond!"

He shook his head. "No, I'm sorry . . . very sorry . . . I'm spoiling your lovely world, old son . . ."

He dropped his eyes and dragged his fingers through the tumbled earth.

"White Lady . . . here!" Lord Sheringham's voice came, curiously loud. "Look! The White Lady!"

Mister Trumpet groaned with the effort of trying to creep into another man's dream. "Where? Where?"

But each man's head is his own castle to which there's no way in at all. Though he be but a yard away, there's lands and forests behind his ordinary eyes where no other man will ever dwell. Marvels he sees with his inward eye—and travels ten thousand miles in the space of a pumpkin! "Look, sir! All the glories, princes, jewels of India: there! In that space at the back of my left eyebrow!"

"What was that?" Mister Trumpet's eyes blazed. "That flash! That glitter! It was the White Lady! I know it! I know her colour! It was she! There!"

"Mister Trumpet! Come back! It was nothing! Moonlight on water! No more! Come back! There's snakes and wild beasts!"

My shouts woke the others. "What is it? Where's he gone?"

We heard him rustling and stamping about, sometime calling on us to follow, then cursing as he caught his foot or scratched his face . . . Mister Morris was for staying where we were—we'd never find him in the tangled, treacherous dark. Wait till dawn. Wait and he'll come back. Men, when they blunder, always come full circle . . . But Lord Sheringham considered, feared the scope of that circle. He might be gone for days . . . more days than he'd strength for . . . he was still sick . . . we could not leave him . . .

"Morris! Morris! Jack!" came Mister Trumpet's voice, echoing eerily. "Over here! Lord Sheringham! The White Lady! It's here!"

So began our great panic, about two hours before first light. Mister Morris was overruled and we gathered our possessions and set off in pursuit of Mister Trumpet's cries.

At first, we went slowly, not daring to separate, and answering his calls with, "Over here! Over here!" or "Stay where you are! Stay still and we'll come!"

Then we began to blunder into tree-trunks and bushes as his voice seemed to come from all sides about us.

"Jack! Morris! Jack! Lord Sheringham!" howled and wailed in the thick dark, sometime above, sometime behind, then in front, as the sound seemed to rebound off the air itself. (I don't think any of us, at that time, had any suspicion of what was happening: indeed, it was days before we knew for certain . . .)

Desperately, we clung together, for the effect of the single madman loose in the night was extraordinarily terrifying. At times, there seemed to be six or seven Mister Trumpets, shouting for each of us in turn: and then another one, some way ahead, rampaging ferociously through the undergrowth, cursing and raging as he went.

I can't remember who was the first of us to break away. Suddenly, I heard Mister Morris's voice, much further off than I'd dreamed he was: Mister Morris's voice, shouting my name, I gripped hard on Lord Sheringham's hand—and pulled at it till he cried out:

"For God's sake, lad—what is it?"

And I found I'd been holding on to Mister Morris himself!

"Where's Lord Sheringham?"

"Here."

He was behind me.

This was the first of half a hundred insane jests of the wicked forest: jests that sent us stumbling, blundering up the side of the unseen slope, drove us into trees till our eyes streamed and scratches made maps of our skin; sent us headlong over roots and creepers; and turning us at last into three wrecked fools who parted with each other's grasping, clutching hands about an hour before the dawn.

Mister Morris kept calling to me. At first, I tried to answer Lord Sheringham, too: but his voice seemed harder to place and I found myself wasting my strength between the two.

So I shut my ears to all but Mister Morris's voice, which was easier to be certain of, owing to his habit of coughing when he was excited.

I came upon him dimly in a clearing, standing as though he was still on a quarter-deck: feet apart, hands cupped to lips, shouting:

"Jack Holborn! Jack! Jack! On deck, lad!"

Then he saw me. "Jack! Where the blazes have you been?"

He was furious: and somehow that shocked me out of my fear of the night and the echoing voices.

"Mister Morris, sir . . . I'm sorry . . . I got lost . . ."

"Jack! Morris! Lord Sheringham! The White Lady! Here!"

Mister Trumpet's voice again, somewhere ahead. First time we'd heard him for close on an hour. He sounded no more than twenty yards off. I tried to follow, when Mister Morris swore at me to stop. Said I'd lose myself again. Said I was off on the wrong tack. Said he'd heard movement to the right, no matter where the voice came from.

"Trumpet! Come quick! I think I've—"

Surely that was Lord Sheringham again—twenty yards ahead? Again Mister Morris held me back.

"The White Lady!"

Where was Lord Sheringham now? Where was he? And what had he found?

"Where are you? Where are you?"

Mister Trumpet suddenly sounded closer than ever—and to the right! We heard him stumble and crash: then at last his half-seen shape lurched past.

"Trumpet!" shouted Mister Morris, and, dragging me by the shoulder, plunged after him.

"The White Lady! Here! Trumpet! Morris! Jack!" How queer Lord Sheringham's voice sounded: thin and excited.

"The White Lady!" shrieked Mister Trumpet—and we fell upon him as he crouched over his wicked treasure! He'd found it, lying in the filth of the forest's floor!

As I looked away into the fading darkness, I thought, for a single instant, of Mister Trumpet's dream—the children—the ever-following, ever-watchful children with their burning black eyes. And I thought of them peering malevolently down through the leaves and branches and shifting shadows: peering and laughing at the poor sick man, who gasped over his heart's stony desire.

"Lord Sheringham!" called Mister Morris, softly. "M'lord!"

But there was no answer. We looked to one another.

"Lord Sheringham! Lord Sheringham!"

Even the echoes were gone.

"Captain!" shouted Mister Morris. "Captain! Where are you?"

He drew breath—then exploded into coughs. Then I shouted—and my voice too died away into the absolute silence that had fallen on the forest. Soon after that, morning came and we knew that we had lost him.

There was no trace, nothing to show where he'd been, or what had become of him. We searched for torn clothing, signs of a struggle, blood: we found nothing. It was as if he'd never existed outside of our minds. This, then, was the first of our two losses in the forest: sudden and frightening.

After the first frenzy of shouting and searching, we sat in a shocked huddle, starting at every rustle of leaves and fancying his faraway cries in the screech and chatter of morning birds.

With the coming of noon, Mister Morris was grey-faced but resolute.

"We must go on," said he. "There's no help for it."

Mister Trumpet looked up from his damned diamond. "You can't mean it, man! We can't leave him!"

"D'you think I want to leave him here? If there was a chance—so small a chance—If I thought . . . I'd . . . We must go on!" he finished abruptly; and stared at his compass, and then to the dark way ahead.

"Listen to me, Morris," said Mister Trumpet, for the first

time putting the White Lady out of sight. "Listen to me. This was my fault. I know it. Mine is all the blame. If not for me—and mine—he'd still be here. So—you take Jack, and go on. I'll wait and search. I'll find him. I feel it: I know it. Go on with Jack, Morris. Go on to the top of your hill."

"Don't play at heroes with me, Mister Trumpet," answered Mister Morris, coldly. "You'll move on with Jack and me. You're a sick man, not capable of feeding yourself, let alone finding the Capt—Lord Sheringham."

Mister Trumpet, instead of flaring up, as he'd have done two days before, took it meekly and bowed his head.

"Morris," he pleaded, "Morris, old friend: let's all stay, then. Let's all wait—just one day more . . ."

But the master shook his neat head. We could not stay. There was no food in this part of the forest. We could not rely on what we might kill: not any longer. We must press on towards ground where the sun fell and ripened edible fruits.

"But—if he should come back . . . and not find us?"

"He'll not come back again." Mister Morris meant what he said: no doubt of it. And his voice was hard as stone.

"Good God!" Mister Trumpet burst out, "You can't mean to abandon a living man so?"

To which Mister Morris replied,

"Didn't *you* hate him? Weren't you ready to kill him once . . . twice?"

"But the agreement, Morris! Our agreement! We've all started anew! The past's no more!"

"Nor is he. There's an end of it."

Now Mister Trumpet roused himself and there was a great deal of courage and anger about him I'd not seen before.

"My mind's made up, Morris. You and Jack must go on alone, I'll stay till I find him. I'll not take another step with you!"

"I—" began Mister Morris; but was spoiled by coughing. When he'd done, he spat and wiped his mouth. "If you don't come, Trumpet, I'll put a ball through your head. I swear it."

He was holding a pistol and levelling it very exactly. Why was he so mad to have Mister Trumpet follow? God knew!

So Mister Trumpet gave in, judging that an ache in his heart was to be preferred to a hole in his head.

So we set off once more, the lonely three of us: and Mister Trumpet's spirits were raised enough for him to sing as he walked—or I thought they were till I realized he was singing to guide Lord Sheringham, wherever he might be.

> *"I'll come back again,*
> *Though I roam ten thousand miles."*

Chapter Fifteen

So he was gone. For two, and maybe three, days I couldn't bring myself to believe it. It didn't seem possible that he wasn't just behind me—or ahead—talking with Mister Morris . . . or anywhere; only, just out of sight—slipped away for the moment . . .

"If only I can count up to a hundred without turning round," I'd promise myself, hopelessly, "he'll be back." And then, when I'd reached that hundred I dared not look back: and went on for another hundred—and cursed myself for waiting too long.

That was how I kept myself going for those first three days: kept myself from abandoning Mister Morris and Mister Trumpet and flying back into the forest to find where he lay and put my hand on his quiet heart and my ear to his quiet lips—and wonder where his promise and my secret was gone.

A thousand excuses I found to delay the little master as he pounded mercilessly ahead: my foot was twisted, a pain in my side, I was weary unto death and could go no further, I'd heard something—seen something—the Lord knew what!—but we must stop.

"Only stop, Mister Morris, sir! For pity's sake, stop just for five minutes!"

But he never did. He knew full well why I'd asked. So I grew to hate him for coming between me and my heart's desire: and the awful battle between us strung and stretched out over the desperate days, waxing with the sun and waning with the night—when even he had to rest. And then he would sit, a compact of prickles and sharpness, staring down at his compass which seemed to hold his soul, and then up into the dark which we must penetrate on the morrow.

I think it was on the fourth day that I gave up my counting, and with it a large part of my hope. Thereafter I settled down to following Mister Morris with a sullen resentment: and found his progress slow. Not for anything, in those days, would I have gone back or loitered. All I wanted was to escape from the foul forest and its endless, endless green.

So it became Mister Trumpet's turn to beg a slower pace—as he wasn't yet fully recovered—though he still sang his unchanging song as loudly as he was able.

"Save your breath for walking," grunted Mister Morris: but Mister Trumpet sang on, and each time his pleasant voice died away among the trees, a look of strained listening would pass across his face. Then he'd smile at me, as if apologising for a weakness . . .

Strange, how kind and generous Mister Trumpet had grown of late: for generous he was to Mister Morris, never provoking him and ever giving way to his harsh ill-temper. He seemed to soften as the other hardened—as if his generosity could only flourish in the face of meanness, and his kindness in the sight of cruelty.

More than once he interposed himself between Mister Morris and me, when, by my thoughtlessness or obstinacy, I'd provoked the little man into a fury: once even receiving a half accidental clout on the side of his head for his pains.

But he took it in good part and next day the mildewed little man was a trifle gentler—but as he wrenched his way through many a scornful thicket and tangle, he seemed to be venting his spleen on the prickly skin of Nature instead.

Sometimes, seeing him scratched to ribbons, and plainly weak on his legs, Mister Trumpet or I would offer to go first for a while: on his directions, of course. But he'd have none of it—not trusting us to take a single step he'd not taken first himself. And even when the forest began to thin and the way was clearer and lighter, he'd stumble on ahead with sometimes his right, and sometimes his left arm outstretched to hold us back. And towards evening, he was so weary that he'd stagger this way and that, like he was drunk. Then Mister Trumpet, motioning me to one side, would again go forward to help him: only to be rebuffed with:

"Look after our food, Trumpet. I'll look after our way."

Eleven days in all we followed him: eleven harsh, dark lonely days; till suddenly, all the signs in Nature showed the little man had led us aright. Everywhere there was evidence of a high place. We were close to the summit of Mister Morris's promontory.

Then, by late afternoon on the twelfth day after the loss of Lord Sheringham (which was the fifteenth following our entry into the great forest), we broke out upon open ground and caught our first sight of Mister Morris's prophecy and dream: the dream that had kept him going so far beyond his ordinary strength; for he was a mildewy man and small, prey to a strong wind and having not much force beyond his own will. We saw the river that henceforth was to be our companion and guide.

Maybe at that time we saw no more than a silver prickle down among the hanging trees: but it was Mister Morris's river and he surveyed it as though it was Jordan.

He paid not much heed to the great wide land he'd brought us to: for the high blue hills and all that lay eastward concerned him not. He studied his river: took out his green leather spy-glass: peered: stared: moved to one side, then another, muttering, sometimes coughing and neglecting to wipe his mouth:

"If she goes thus—and thus . . . if there be no rapids . . . she's wide . . . wide already . . . broad and fine! Maybe deep enough for—ten, fifteen miles . . . They could build a raft . . . What's that? Overhanging rocks . . . on the bank . . . Thank God . . . a most excellent river . . . a gentle, gentle current . . ."

He put away his glass and laid his compass on the ground. I never saw him do that before: let go his compass, I mean. Then he turned and came back up the hill: for in his excitement he'd gone a little way off.

"Morris! You're bleeding!" said Mister Trumpet suddenly: for there was blood trickling out of the side of his mouth, and several stains on his chin from where he'd been coughing. For the first time, I looked hard at Mister Morris's face in the sunlight, and saw that it was extraordinarily pale—greyish, rather . . .

But he shook his head impatiently and bade us sit down while he outlined his plan. No more need for compass and sextant. Just follow the river. Maybe build a raft? but better, walk by the banks. Take shelter at noon, for two or three hours, when the sun's hottest . . .

"For God's sake don't walk in the sun. And beware of bathing in the river, for fear of crocodiles.

"And when you reach the port—for there *will* be a port where this fine river joins the sea—pick the home-bound ship with care. Choose a ship that's not too high in the poop (like the Spaniards), but of a low, clean line. And don't trust the new craft that carry overmuch canvas. They'll not ride out the gales. Beware of a ship too heavily laden: for there's greed in the owners and foolishness in the captain to allow such a thing."

"But this is your affair, Morris," put in Mister Trumpet, uneasily, "the choice of a ship lies in your hands."

"Remember the *Charming Molly* and what befell her," went on Mister Morris, signing Mister Trumpet to be silent. "Therefore, look to her cannon. No less than twelve, and polished well: which is a sign of gunners who are men of good trade.

"And remember that, in the last resort, a ship depends on her crew. Therefore, I say, avoid like the plague mealy-mouthed pigs who, when they drink, talk vilely of their wives and homes. For such men have no great wish to return and are likely to mutiny.

"And—and though you are rich, pay no more than the next man for your passage. You may be shrewd, Solomon Trumpet, but you're no match for a belaying-pin in the dark. And—where would your White Lady be then? And—"

Here he was broke off by the most violent fit of coughing he ever had, and I saw he brought up a good deal of frothy blood.

"We'd best remain till tomorrow," murmured Mister Trumpet. "Till Morris here has recovered."

"You'll go now!" spluttered Mister Morris, fiercely. "Now! *Now*, I say!"

"But you're not fit, man!"

"I—remain—here!"

"You're out of your mind! We can't leave you!"

"For the last time, Mister Trumpet: you must obey me. For God's sake—begone!"

He tried to get up: struggled like a horse with a snapped neck. But his strength was spent and he fell back, choking and spitting to keep the continuous blood out of his mouth. We flew to help him—and he fought to keep us away. His chest was paining him dreadfully. Mister Trumpet drew aside his shirt. For the first time we saw the "bruising" he'd suffered. The bruising!

Since the wreck of the *Charming Molly* he'd been carrying a splinter of the shattered helm clean into his lung! He must have guessed from the first he was done for, yet he'd kept himself going—and kept his horrible secret. All he'd desired was to get us to safety.

Very much ashamed was I to recall hating him for his short temper: for it was only matching itself to the shortness of his life.

"Now you know," said he, quietly. "There's nothing to be done but leave me. And quickly—quickly! God! Even the wretches at Tyburn are given a last wish! Would you deny me that?"

"We'd deny you nothing, Mister Morris," said Mister Trumpet, softly. "Save that. We cannot leave you . . ."

"Fools! Damned, damned fools!" raged Mister Morris, weakly. "Wasting time—wasting—"

His head fell back into the crook of Mister Trumpet's arm. Strange, how his strength ebbed so suddenly now his aim was achieved . . .

There was no sense in deceiving such a man as Mister Morris that he was likely to live. It would have robbed him of his dignity: and at such a time, that's all a man has . . .

"When we get back," murmured Mister Trumpet. "Is there anything . . . anyone . . .?"

"No-one." He attempted a smile: the first I'd seen on him since the loss of Lord Sheringham—but had it cut off.

"I'm glad to see the—the sky again. Thought I—I mightn't . . . would like to've seen the sea, but—

"Trumpet: you're not a bad fellow, y'know, now your fever's cured. Know what I mean? And Jack—Jack Holborn—be capable . . . learn a trade . . . learn it well . . . self-respect . . . very important . . . do—do one thing well, eh? Be—"

He was having such difficulty in keeping his eyes open that it was terrible to watch him. Mister Trumpet scowled and bit his lip at the harshness of nature in her manner of cutting off; that she should let the spirit know so much of the failing of the flesh.

"Jack!" cried Mister Morris, suddenly excited. "Jack Holborn! Give—give me your hand—"

I did so; and soon after that he was dead, without ever having uttered another word.

Afterwards, we knelt and looked down on him for more minutes than I can tell. This was the saddest moment in all my life: to see him lying there, small, still, and with all the quickness gone out of his face, so it was no more than nose, mouth and chin which might have been any dead man's, and were not any more—nor ever again would be—mildewed Mister Morris's.

We would have buried him on the peak of his promontory, but the ground was too hard: so we went down a way and dug him a grave in the shadow of the trees, and not far from his river. For decency's sake, we made it as deep as we were able (about four feet), and covered his face with his shirt before we filled it in. When it was done, we smoothed over the earth with our hands so there should be no cause for anybody who came thereafter to dig in that place again.

We left about an hour before nightfall, and went down towards the river to wash the grave-mud from our hands. Mister Trumpet carried the extra jewel-bag and I took the compass, spyglass and knife. The sextant we abandoned as it was of no more use to us.

Chapter Sixteen

THE first day and night of the world from which Mister Morris was gone. It was not very changed. The sun still set— and came up again. Mister Trumpet was by my side, and I was by his. We were still rich: exceedingly rich. We were on our way home. And Mister Morris's river would guide us.

What did it matter if we were ragged, hungry, bush-torn—
and short of two companions? All we'd to do was to walk
(but not in the noonday sun: last words to be honoured!)
and walk and never look back. There was no cause for anything but thankfulness . . .

But by the end of that first four and twenty hours, rich as
I was, I'd fallen into a despair from which neither Mister
Trumpet nor my jewels could lift me.

I suppose it was the river, from which I'd expected one
thing and now found another. With its discoverer gone, I lost
all faith in it. That first fine glimpse had been a piece of silver
treachery.

It was an abominable river: a river that ran directly out of
the sun to wind its uncanny way through the dark of the
world. Never far, never near, it beckoned with its muddy
miles to God knew where.

By day, its colour was yellow—from the mud of its bed—
and flecked and speckled by a veil of flies. By night, it was
black. And yet once, glimpsed through the trees, it had sparkled
like a necklace!

Our companion and guide: our highroad: our arrow of
salvation: a creeping hearse of dead branches, and rotted vege-
tation, endlessly slit by the sinful smile of crocodiles.

By nightfall on the second day we had reached a point where
a south-bound slave-train came out of the eastern forest. For
us, this was a moment of triumph and a sign of great hope:
for men with merchandise must be bound for a port.

It was about a hundred and twenty strong, moving in
double file and fork-yoked front to back and chained cross-
wise. Providing the black men walked submissively and in
step, they could not have been vastly uncomfortable: but
escape was never possible. The whole was in the charge of
seven Arabs, who took it in turn to ride in the two ox-carts
that accompanied the procession. This seemed to me a better
way of travelling than on our sore feet. (For I never forgot we

were millionaires.) But Mister Trumpet looked at me as if I was mad and said we'd be safer on the backs of the crocodiles. With our riches, he said, he'd not trust an Englishman, let alone seven slavers.

It was on the evening of the fifteenth day after Mister Trumpet's burning children, and the fourteenth after we last saw Lord Sheringham, that we came to overlook the south-bound slave-train: and it was on that same evening that those two circumstances caught up with us, so to speak, and lived again in the eye of Mister Morris's spyglass.

I was dreaming: an agreeable dream, I fancy, for I was irritable with Mister Trumpet for knocking me out of it . . . He was hunched and staring through the spyglass at the line of small fires that lit the drowsing slave-train.

"The children, Jack! D'you see? The children of my dream! Look! Look!"

He passed me the glass. I said he was mad. He said, "maybe", and begged me to look. So I did.

I saw: five Arabs by one of the fires. Standing. Whips stuck out behind them, like devils' tails. In the firelight. Surprised bellies swelling out their gowns, like mainsails in a stout breeze.

And Mister Trumpet's burning children. Seven. Dark against the flames. Armed with small spears and blow-pipes. Heads as high as the Arab bellies. Not an inch more. Mannikins!

"Pygmies!" whispered Mister Trumpet. "Why did we never guess? Pygmies!"

"And that's what you saw? In your fever?"

"Yes. Looking down on me, through the leaves."

"Why? Why? What did they want?"

He had the glass off me again and stared more towards the back of the fire—to the darker shadows—as if he knew what he was looking for but had not yet found it. Then he gave a great sigh and gave me back the glass.

"It needs younger eyes," he breathed. "Tell me what you

H

see in the outer shadows. Take your time—and tell me . . . exactly . . . what you see . . . missing nothing . . ."

I took the glass and looked.

I saw: "A man, Mister Trumpet. A pale-skinned man."

"Wearing?"

"Wearing a—a torn white shirt, Mister Trumpet. I think he is bound and gagged. His mouth seems covered . . ."

"Of what age, Jack? What's his colouring?"

"A little past middle-age, Mister Trumpet. Grey-haired, with a washed-out country complexion."

"His name, Jack? His name is—?"

"Lord Sheringham, Mister Trumpet. Lord Sheringham!"

The shock and joy we felt were indescribable. For we'd been sure he was dead. It was a very wonderful moment to see him there—far below us—unmistakably still in the world. Much separated him from us, vast difficulties and obstacles, no doubt: but they could be as nothing compared with what we'd thought. No distance could have been as great as that: no obstacle as huge as the small flat stone that marks a grave. For in life, all things are possible: and he was alive! My secret was alive—and, therefore, his promise, still waiting to be won.

From then on we watched, through the spyglass, a most remarkable sequence of events.

I saw the Traders, nervous of the blowpipes, eye the valuable rare little men greedily, as if they were several hundred independent guineas, walking the night unpocketed.

But they kept their distance, and presently squatted, cross-legged, with expansive gestures that said: "We will talk business." Then I gave up the spyglass.

And the business was this: the pygmies had come to sell the Judge. Not for money, but for a captured pygmy woman who was brought forward into the firelight.

Back and forth went the bargainers among themselves: impossible to say what passed, but the essence was plain. The

Slavers wanted more than the Judge for their pygmy. For maybe an hour they argued, drank with one another, then resumed. At last, a bargain was struck. A hard one. Two articles for one. One of the pygmy warriors gave up his weapons, embraced his friends, and, together with Lord Sheringham, went into slavery. If his heart was broken at the loss of his forests, we never heard the sound of it. A grave and careful young man of great good manners and courtesy. Then the captive woman was freed and the hunting party departed with their costly purchase to a point along the river's bank where rock and silted mud made a shallow ford.

I thought we'd seen and heard the last of them; but their way back to their own far-off forests passed close by where we lay. They were joyful as they scrambled by, despite the loss of a friend. (Maybe they never cared much for him?) They shouted and played children's games on one another—imitating birds and beasts (very proficiently, for that's how they hunted—by decoying), the voices and gestures of the Arabs, and other voices, they imitated, too . . .

They looked down to the slave-camp and cried out:

"Jack! Mister Trumpet! Lord Sheringham! White Lady! Here!"

Then they shrieked and shrieked with derisive laughter. Mister Trumpet and me looked to one another, violently astonished. The voice that came from the mimicking pygmy lips was the voice of dead Mister Morris!

Long, long after they'd gone, we lay there, Mister Trumpet and me, thinking and wondering and whispering till we knew for certain-sure, how thoroughly and abominably we'd been tricked. From the first, from the very first, we surmised . . .

They must have seen us wrecked and come to land on that blazing morning—that hunting party scouring the forest for something to trade for their stolen companion. How anxiously they must have watched us deliberate our plan—the Captain, Mister Morris, Mister Trumpet and me: for they'd a plan of their own . . .

"D'you remember the uncanny signs across the swamp? They must have laid them to lead us on!"

"I remember," said Mister Trumpet, half-admiringly—for he could not but admire anyone who outwitted him, conceiving how difficult that must be—"I remember . . . and once or twice I wondered . . . but—"

Their plan must have been to lead us to where they might separate us most easily. That way they'd save themselves the trouble of carrying a captive over difficult country. Then, when we'd obligingly walked the worst for them, they'd capture one (they weren't greedy, and two might have proved an embarrassment)—they'd capture the one who seemed most valuable.

And we could scarce have been more obliging if we'd tried. Mister Trumpet and his White Lady. To pygmy eyes, it must have appeared like a small god. They knew he'd go mad to get it back. And they knew we'd follow him. (Hadn't they followed their lost one?) Rightly, they estimated our loyalty to be stronger than our sense.

And then, as they were wont to trap game by mimicry, luring beasts from their herds by false calls, so they lured and separated us. They panicked us in the forest as if we'd been beasts! And when their time was ripe, we fell. Lord Sheringham was alone. Down from the trees they plummeted, stifled his voice and bound him—and dropped the White Lady where he'd stood. (Maybe they'd dropped it first, so's he'd stoop to pick it up?) For they'd no use for the little shining thing. And who knew its powers? It might have brought them bad luck!

Later—much later—I found it in my heart to forgive them for what they'd done to us. I came to understand that their need had been as acute as mine; and I respected their forbearance in leaving us unharmed. A thousand times they could have killed us with their blowpipes: but they let us live. A gentle people who never killed but for food: and we, thank God! were not appetizing.

So I forgave them their cunning: but what I could never forgive them was the thin, measly, weedy sound they made which Mister Trumpet recognized as a skilful imitation of my agreeable voice. That, I could not forgive at all.

Chapter Seventeen

WE followed the slave-train for more than twelve days, keeping a distance of half a mile by day, and drawing closer at night. Sometimes, it wound through forest land, sometimes along the river bank.

Then, on the thirteenth day, shortly before dusk, Lord Sheringham, still yoked with slaves, trudged into the independent port of N—. Sure was never a stranger journey taken by an English judge! For thirteen days he'd walked, slept, eaten and dwelt like a poor beast of burden: no better. His spirit had been subjected to all the slow fires of shame and disaster, and his flesh had been mortified by whips. What had it done to him? Had his spirit hardened against oppression? Or had it failed? Had his pride leaped above the whips? Or had it crouched beneath them? For nothing stands still. Not even in such an one as he.

We saw him locked up in a compound together with some hundreds of reeking, sunk-chested black men whose boot-bright skin ran as if it was weeping. We left him there, beside the pygmy, who, willy-nilly, had been his constant companion.

For a moment, I thought he'd seen us—for he was looking our way—but many tangled bodies crossed and re-crossed between, and Mister Trumpet said it was not so, and dragged

me off into the darkening heart of the town: being anxious
to sell some jewels.

"Money, Jack! Money! We must have money!"

So we went in search of money, did Mister Trumpet and me,
hand in hand: for, by God! I'd never have let go of him in
such a place as the independent port of N—.

The extreme of poverty made even the countless children
and the scanty aged dangerous with despair. This was the
bottom of the world where ulcered feet trod on beating necks
to crawl up out of it.

Down the mud that ran between the huts we went, and,
like a pair of tattered moths, made for wherever there shone
a light. But lights seemed to belong to those who were only
rich enough to light their poverty . . .

And all through this terrible place flickered the same hope,
gleaming in many a yellowed eye that, maybe, longed only to
be closed. For hereabouts men dwelt at their lowest ebb, living
by the second, dying by the hour, and depending for their
quickening on—changes in the wind, a bird out of season, a
pair of tattered strangers such as Mister Trumpet and me . . .
In short, anything out of the ordinary: for the ordinary was—
despair.

"Lord! Mister Trumpet, we'll find no money here!"

But we did. At the back of the waterfront. A white-painted
wooden shack with a raised-up porch around it.

We found Mister Thompson; a black man who kept a store
for the benefit of drunk sailors to dispose of whatever they'd
got left: and for the black King of N— who'd sometimes take
it into his shiny head to sally out and buy one of his dozen
black wives some brocaded silk that he'd heard Mister Thompson had newly imported.

Stranger sights than us had met Mister Thompson's bulging
eyes, so our ragged condition never put him off for an instant.
Even when Mister Trumpet held out a middle-sized ruby, he
was not surprised. Nothing surprised Mister Thompson. If all

the independent port of N— had vanished in a puff of sulphur and smoke, Mister Thompson would not have been surprised. He smiled at Mister Trumpet's ruby.

"Twenty pound," he said. "Sir!"

"It's worth a thousand!" exclaimed Mister Trumpet, angrily.

"In Lisbon, or London; maybe. Here—twenty pound: sir!"

"Are rubies so plentiful here, Mister Thompson? Do they grow on your rotting trees that they should be so cheap?"

"No."

"Then why so little?"

"Get more if you can: sir! Maybe a ship's captain give you twenty-five? Thirty? Fifty, even? And maybe he knocks you on the head and gets it for nothing? Sir! Upon the other hand, I give you twenty pound and no knock on the head. I promise: sir! Leave it—or take it!"

"You're a hard man, Mister Thompson," sighed Mister Trumpet, half smiling. Mister Thompson seemed to appeal to his sense of business.

"Me, hard? Oh, sir! Never! Look—" He prodded his fat, cushiony fingers into his forearm where they sank into his fat flesh. "Soft as butter! Twenty pound: sir!"

He held up the ruby to his lamp and admired its fine colour. He glanced approvingly at Mister Trumpet. The gentleman didn't bring rubbish.

"What if we take goods, Mister Thompson?"

"Choose: sir!"

So we chose: clothes. Not very splendid ones, for Mister Thompson's stock was limited to the very second-hand, bought off unlucky seamen and robbed passengers, and bore many signs of unsteady meals at sea.

But we managed, rummaging among bales behind the counter, watched sideways by gleaming-toothed Mister Thompson. Mister Trumpet did better than me, turning out rather well in grey breeches and a green coat with most of its gilt buttons. But the "young gentleman" came off rather queerly in blue and cream made for a bigger man altogether.

"Now," said Mister Trumpet, at length, straightening himself in his finery, "how much for this?"

He held out a small emerald. Mister Thompson barely glanced at it and said: "Two hundred guineas: sir!"

"But it's worth less than the ruby!"

Mister Thompson shrugged his elephant shoulders.

"I was lucky, there, sir! I bought the ruby from a ragged beggar who had no choice. Needed money badly. Poor devil: sir! The emerald I buy from a gentleman who might go elsewhere in his fine clothes. Therefore—two hundred guineas: sir!

"Perhaps you get two hundred and five elsewhere? but I think not. Not in N—. Now you have what you need. Enough to pay passage home and there sell the remainder of jewels you hide in your linen bag: sir!

"Oh, sir! you'll be rich! And a gentleman, too! I knew it at once! As soon as I saw the ruby, I said to myself, 'Mister Thompson, there's a proper gentleman, only needing a bit of money to be translated. Mister Thompson, you let him have a little for the first stone and he'll dress himself up and come again. Then give him more for the second stone, and he'll respect you for it! Oh, yes, he'll think to himself "Though Mister Thompson is fat and smelly and has a black face, he knows what's what and is as proper a gentleman as me myself." ' That's what I say to myself: eh, sir!"

We spent the rest of the night in Mister Thompson's shop, for he'd a bolt on the door and we'd come to trust him. If he stole any of our jewels in the night, they must have been small ones, for we never missed them. And in the morning, he provided us with a breakfast of fruit and eggs for which we paid him sixpence—according to his own demand.

We asked him about the slave auction, and he told us it was to be held mid-morning and would be finished quickly as there were only two ships in harbour and both anxious to be off.

"The flies . . . the poor men go mad with the flies . . ."

Mister Trumpet asked him if he'd join us but—"no, he'd not

come to the compound with us. Once, he'd been unlucky . . .
lost a nephew (brother's child), for seven pound ten. Bid eight,
but not heard. Gentleman said it was wrong for a black man
to buy his own kind: not gentlemanly. And what had we in
mind? House slaves—or for the land? Always look to their
teeth, gentlemen. The teeth have it. No teeth: no eat. Very
soon grow thin and die. Wasted guineas. But maybe rich
gentlemen don't mind wasting guineas?"

When we said it was a white man we wanted, a friend of
ours, he nodded and said it was a fine thing to put money to—
"to buy a friend . . . not many times done . . . but maybe we
were rich enough even for that? Only, look to his teeth. Black
or white, the teeth have it. No sense in buying a friend who'd
go rotten and perish on the way home . . ."

Before we left he gave us best advice:

"Not too eager, sirs. Let it seem you're prepared to let him
go to a higher bidder. For they'll cheat you, will the Arabs.
Not proper gentlemen. Let it be, 'Ah! he's worth no more to
me! Regrets, gentlemen. A friend's a friend: but money's
money. Take him. My heart breaks—but not my pocket.' Let
them think you're hard. They'll respect you for it: sirs!

"And—and if it goes against you—for I can see the young
gentleman might be over anxious—never worry. Next time
do better. A friend lost: money saved. Always think: may get
a better friend next time—cheaper. Learn from experience."

He smiled at Mister Trumpet: "We know, eh? Sir! Look
after the young gentleman. And come back when you're done.
If you've bought anything, Mister Thompson will fit him out
reasonable! And if you've been unlucky, Mister Thompson
will comfort. Very comfortable, Mister Thompson."

So we left Mister Thompson's by mid-morning for the
sweaty crowds and fly-blown sunshine of N—, where sailors
and passengers from the two ships in harbour wandered curiously, looking their fill on the worst place in the world:
wondering how much they could buy for how little, seeking
out the poorest to cheat them the most easily.

But we were to seek out a gentleman called Ibram Fared, who was neither poor nor easily to be cheated. A man of great importance in N—, without whom not so much as a child might be sold. A man through whose lean, brown hands all the marketable flesh of that part of the coast was wont to pass. A man whose eye was keener than any physician's in judging of health and strength and expectancy of life, which he measured to the nearest shilling.

If a slave knew Mister Fared had sold him for sixpence, he died within the week: for he knew Mister Fared had looked into his heart and seen it would not beat beyond such a day. So he died. No-one cheated Mister Fared: not even in so small a way as that.

It was from Mister Fared, then, that we must buy Lord Sheringham. Mister Trumpet sighed and looked grim: like a soldier about to go into battle. But I was more hopeful . . .

Chapter Eighteen

I'M done with auctions. I'll never go to another as long as I live. This is my own desire and Mister Trumpet's definite advice. He says I'm no good at them. A danger. He says I betray every single jot of feeling from anxiety to flat panic: that my face is as plain as a ledger with profit and loss shown in red and white and a total forever in my unbuttoned mouth. He says he'd never trust me near an auction unless I was in armour with the vizor down. And even then, he wonders . . .

Yet what did I do wrong? At what point did disaster begin? I obeyed him exactly, until I had my flash of wisdom. But by then it was too late . . .

122

And all seemed to be going so well. Even Mister Trumpet had thought things were going well. Mister Fared, the formidable Mister Fared, proved to be no more than a courteous, elderly gentleman, very punctilious in his bargaining: the two sea-captains who were there seemed plain enough, honest enough fellows: and even Sir Joseph Downs (part-owner of Captain Farmer's ship), didn't seem so bad an English gentleman.

I blame Mister Trumpet for his foolish agreement with Sir Joseph. That's where disaster lay. I've never trusted those great fat men with loud voices and fair hair. They've too much an air of command about them—and too little an air of authority.

To save bidding against each other, *he* was going to bid for us. It would save money. *He'd* do the bidding. He'd a loud voice and was used to cattle auctions in Worcestershire. He knew his way about. I saw Mister Trumpet nod, and then make a private resolve to take things out of his large, hairy hands if things should go awry. And I made a similar resolve.

Not that Sir Joseph wanted the shrunk, dismal-looking white man who was Lord Sheringham, the great judge. It was on account of the pygmy. The pygmy was still shackled to him. They were one lot. Oddments. One valuable, the other worthless: depending on what you collected—judges or mannikins.

So Mister Fared stood to gain from whoever wanted either. And the purchaser had to pay for what he didn't want. Nobody could have wanted both.

So that's how it came about: Mister Trumpet's too clever agreement.

We got to the compound early—too early by half: for a second train had come in during the night and had been rubbed down with oil to make the black men look shinier and healthier than they were. The smell was horrible. And the oil attracted the flies in wicked, speckled clouds.

Not being horses, the slaves had no tails to flick off their tormentors, so they kept twisting and turning and waving their heavily shackled arms to keep themselves clear. They looked like they were dancing: but there were six hundred of them in not much space, and they kept falling and being jerked up by neighbours' chains, and yelping with the sudden pain of it.

Our slave-train suffered too: but not so much for they were free of the oil.

Sir Joseph Downs made over towards us from Mister Fared's verandah as soon as he saw where we were making for. There was no time for anything of greeting, astonishment or delight between Lord Sheringham and us before Sir Joseph was on us and put a stop to it. ("Don't be too eager, young man. Fared can see you. The price'll rise . . .")

"I've already warned him," muttered Mister Trumpet, sourly.

I'd only just got to him with a "We've come for you! It's all right now! You're saved!" whispered very quiet: and a quick look into his scorched face with its wrinkles left like scars, marking old laughter lines . . . Then a moment's panic when he looked blank and I thought he'd lost his memory, before he smiled and I was all right again—and I called to Mister Trumpet that he was all right and we'd come in time—

That's all. That's all there was time for when we were interrupted and Mister Trumpet overreached himself with his shrewd agreement.

As soon as Sir Joseph saw we didn't want the pygmy, he was all over friendly and came quickly to terms with Mister Trumpet. A price was fixed and only one would bid. Four hundred guineas, if need be: two hundred each.

So it was arranged, d'you see, between them before ever we went into that dark, dark hut of Mister Fared's: before ever the first bid was made for the pair of oddments left out in the sun.

"Fifty guineas."

The rest was over and done with: the Portuguese captain, dark as the Arab, had bought most. I thought he'd finished;

overspent himself; he sat so quiet he might have been asleep.

"Fifty guineas."

He spoke good English. Fifty guineas *is* good English. Mister Fared smiled. It was good Arabic, too. He looked to Captain Farmer, to Mister Trumpet, to Sir Joseph. Not a sound.

"Fifty guineas?" (Maybe it wasn't such good Arabic?)

Why didn't Sir Joseph speak? I admit I got a bit worried then—when he hung on for so long I thought he'd been struck dumb and we'd lose all because of his misfortune: but I didn't, as Mister Trumpet afterward affirmed, pluck at his coat and tell him to "speak up! We've got the money!"

"Sixty," said Sir Joseph, very offhandedly; and looked round the hut as if he'd like it better cleaned.

Another silence: and I felt Mister Fared's eyes scrape across me—like a cobweb in the dark, almost.

"Seventy." The Portuguese creaked in his chair to look out through the open door to where his goods fought the tormenting flies. He seemed more interested in them than in his guineas. He watched to see if they were still strong enough to defend themselves: to see they didn't give up and hang down from their chains and let the flies eat them up . . .

"Ninety." Sir Joseph bid quicker now—as if there was a hidden rhythm in it all that he was tuned to and came in on its beat. Like the rhythm outside where the slaves had started their singing in the hope it would keep off the flies.

"One hundred and ten guineas." The Portuguese had got out a small, cruel knife and was cleaning the sweaty dirt from under his fingernails. Mister Fared leaned over and offered him a toothpick for the purpose. The Portuguese smiled and shook his head. Till the bargaining was over, all men were polite enemies. No gifts, not even a toothpick. Captain Farmer nodded approvingly.

"And thirty!" spoke Sir Joseph. I was relieved. He'd let it go long that time. But all was going well. Mister Trumpet looked unconcerned—leaning against the wall, whistling with his red lips alone. (I knew the air: oh! I guessed the air!)

Again I caught Mister Fared's cobwebby glance. I looked away quick. I didn't want to betray anything. I looked out unconcernedly to the compound.

"A hundred and fifty guineas!" He used perfume, did the Portuguese: heavy, sickly stuff that made my head swim.

How well did he know Mister Fared? I thought I caught an odd look between them. And Captain Farmer, too. There'd been something of a glance between him and the Portuguese: and between him and Mister Fared. Nothing much . . . but I wondered. I began to think the three of them might be together against Sir Joseph—and us.

"Two hundred guineas!" Sir Joseph spoke much louder now. Very commanding: very much "end of this nonsensing". Mister Fared spread his hands and shook his thin head imperceptibly, as if to say he understood Sir Joseph was a large man and large men must have their way: but he could not answer for the Portuguese gentleman who, maybe, wasn't gentlemanly enough to see things his and Sir Joseph's way. He was powerless. It was the way of the world. A wicked world: but, alas, the only one . . .

I began to understand that Mister Fared was not quite so simple as he was courteous. I began to understand his smiles and silences and tickling glances were louder by far than Sir Joseph's—or his rivals'—voices.

"Two hundred and fifty guineas."

"You see," Mister Fared's strange penetrating eyes seemed to say—not so much to Sir Joseph, as to me—"it was impossible to stop him. What can I do? Believe me, it pains me . . ."

Mister Trumpet beckoned to me: tried to drag me away from Mister Fared's huge eyes.

"Then—three hundred guineas!" Sir Joseph glanced back to Mister Trumpet whose look never seemed to change.

I tried to sort out what was happening between them. It was beyond me. Battalions of guineas were duelling it out in the dark hut under their subtle commanders.

I'd have gone outside to clear my head, but the heat was

blinding. (And he was out in it! I heard a man screaming—not with pain, but with agony from the flies.)

"Three hundred and fifty."

They were still at it. Still! Still being wickedly shrewd and evilly clever. Still stabbing each other in the pocket. But they'd never bleed from such wounds. It takes iron shackles to draw blood . . .

"Four hundred guineas."

We'd reached the limit. Sir Joseph had done it. It was finished. So sure was I of that, that it came as a dreadful shock when the Portuguese capped it with:

"Four hundred and fifty."

I didn't believe him.

Sir Joseph looked again to Mister Trumpet. Why didn't Mister Trumpet nod? What was another hundred to us? Or, rather, fifty? Sir Joseph was paying half.

"Go on," I whispered. "It's all right!"

(I did speak then: but why not?)

"Five hundred, then?" Mister Fared suggested very kindly, very helpfully. Mister Trumpet shook his head at me: but managed a smile—of sorts. Then he nodded.

"Five hundred guineas," said Sir Joseph: but he didn't seem in command any more. Some hundred guineas over which he'd no authority had suddenly appeared under his banner. Could he count on them?

"Six hundred," said the damned Portuguese; and laid his knife on the table. He'd nicked his finger and sucked at it. *He* was bleeding, anyway.

"Go on, Mister Trumpet," I muttered. "Finish it!"

"Quiet, Jack!"

"I won't be quiet! You can't let him go!"

"For God's sake—"

"Keep that boy—"

"A thousand guineas? A thousand guineas, Mister Fared!" That was my bid. I'd seen Mister Fared was getting too interested in our discussion. So I stopped it.

"Come, young gentleman," Mister Fared smiled encouragingly. "We may all say 'a thousand guineas', or 'ten thousand', or 'twenty thousand'. And a fine ring it has. But what does it *mean*? Here we are all honest men of business. Our word is our bond. When we say 'a thousand', we mean it. We have a thousand. Now: have you a thousand? Have your friends a thousand?"

"Tell him, Mister Trumpet!"

Mister Trumpet had no choice. He went somewhat grey.

"We have the thousand."

"So the bid stands?"

"A thousand guineas."

Sir Joseph was alarmed. He began to bluster a bit. (That's where the damage was done, I'll swear. Not with me at all. If only Sir Joseph had kept his head!)

He'd been forced higher than he'd intended. Our agreement. Too heavily committed.

"One thousand and four hundred guineas!"

The Portuguese was not to be stopped. He'd set his heart on the pygmy. (Maybe for a duchess in Lisbon?) He was sweating now, and it didn't mix well with his scent. The hut was grown nearly as reeking as the compound. And we were only six—not counting the guineas. But at least we were spared the dreadful flies.

"Eighteen hundred." Mister Trumpet was prompt. Too prompt.

"One thousand and eight hundred guineas?"

"Yes."

"Forgive me sir,—but may we, ah, see it? You understand, of course—no offence—not questioning your honour—but bids made in the heat—all too easy—don't want friends to fall out over—hm!—exaggerations—men of business—money on the table, so to speak, eh? Foolish to go on—laughable—Must, regret *must* see it."

"Stay here!" muttered a desperate Mister Trumpet to me. "Stay here! I'll be back!"

He was off to Mister Thompson's to make another sale. To Mister Fared he flung: "I'll fetch it: directly!"

The Arab bowed his head and hid his spreading smile. Then Mister Trumpet was gone and I left alone. The hut was held at bay by the eighteen hundred points of Mister Trumpet's promised guineas.

I saw him hurry past the compound. I wondered if he'd turn and wave. He did: into the compound. And all the slaves waved back. All of them. Raised their hooped arms and shouted to him. "Master!" he said the word was. They thought he'd bought them all and were begging for kind treatment. He clapped his hands to his ears—and ran.

"This is wrong—badly done—to halt in the middle—" the Portuguese was muttering, almost to himself. Yet Mister Fared looked up sharply.

What was happening? Mister Trumpet was gone. Power, force had shifted. Sir Joseph was not of much account on his own. He was not as formidable as the slender, quiet, negligent Mister Trumpet. Not so much to be reckoned with.

"Not the way to do business: I bid fourteen hundred . . . have it here—with me—"

"Five minutes," murmured Mister Fared. "Five minutes grace—courtesy—gentlemen—"

"Fourteen hundred guineas," repeated the Portuguese, growing harder and looking peculiarly at Sir Joseph.

Sir Joseph felt himself to be held to ransom by the Portuguese: shifted—would have escaped—looked to catch Captain Farmer's eye, (for some support). Captain Farmer avoided him. Didn't want to be dragged in.

"Fourteen hundred, I said!"

The Portuguese glanced quickly to Captain Farmer to see if he'd interfere. Some thoughts passed between them. Captain Farmer's eyes dropped to his clasped hands. Never saw Sir Joseph's big, embarrassed pleading. Unlucky.

"The last offer was eighteen hundred, sir," murmured Mister Fared.

"Where?"

"Here!" said I.

Mister Fared nodded. The Portuguese jeered.

"A child! A child's bid! Fourteen hundred, it stands at!"

"Four minutes more—"

The Portuguese stood up. A cannon might have exploded: so sudden was the effect.

"No way to do business. No way at all. I'll buy nothing. Nothing."

"*Nothing?*" Mister Fared was thrown off balance. "But—but our agreement? The others are sold to you—gentleman's word—"

"No way to do business," repeated the Portuguese, seizing his advantage. "I'll not deal with a man who cheats at a sale."

"*Cheats?* No! No! Never!"

"*This* is cheating: to hold up the auction! To be deaf to an honourable bid!"

"Three minutes more—"

"Am I dealing with a rogue—or an honest man? For I'll buy nothing from a rogue!" He looked about him: picked on the weakest point—Sir Joseph. "You, sir! Can you pay eighteen hundred guineas?"

Sir Joseph lost his head. Disclaimed. No part of the bargain. Only just met Mister Trumpet. Didn't know him.

Mister Fared glanced very savagely at Sir Joseph. The gentleman should not have spoken: should have held his tongue.

Sir Joseph was in a panic. (Somehow, he'd still failed to catch Captain Farmer's eye.) What if he should be forced to pay up? Terrible. Impossible. A monstrous situation: not of his making. He threw in his hand.

"I agree! I agree! Fared must accept the bid! No-one's here to cap it! He must accept! It's the way of things. My vote's for the foreign captain there! An honest man. Right's on his side!"

Mister Fared was weakening. I could see he was weakening. His hut was full of angels and devils. Which was which? I had to do something. Even Mister Trumpet would have granted that.

That was when I took the emerald from my linen bag. (It was the first stone that came to hand.)

"What will you give me for—this?"

For a moment, no-one heard. Then a silence fell on the hut. Mister Fared stretched out his hand. He took the stone: stared into it: weighed it: touched his teeth and cheek on it: tasted it—

"A hundred guineas, young sir?"

"Don't cheat the boy, Fared!" Captain Farmer spoke up suddenly. His eyes had gone as green as the jewel. "It's worth two hundred of any man's money!"

"You talk of cheating?" Mister Fared was hurt. "It's worth a thousand—in London: and—five hundred here!" He stared at my linen bag. How many more inside?

I looked to see if Mister Trumpet was in sight. I couldn't hold them off much longer. I felt the weight of them pressing down on me. My hands sweated so's I could scarcely hold my bag. No sign of Mister Trumpet. Nothing but the black men in the sun: some singing, some still doing their weird noisy dance, to keep off the flies: some hanging listless in their chains, content to be a meal.

Back in the hut, power was still with the emerald.

"I—I cannot decide, gentlemen—"

"Fourteen hundred! Sell!"

"He's right! Right's on his side!"

"Time . . . a little time . . ."

"No!"

"Two minutes—on my honour—"

"No! Time's run out! Time has run out!"

And it was then that I had my extraordinary flash of wisdom.

Just as the hut was fallen into chaos. Just as the web of under-standing and cross-understanding broke into a million angry pieces under the weight of my emerald. Everything stood suddenly clear.

It was as if I was light as air: and the four lumpish bargainers bulked like wood in the dark of the hut—slow, peevish blocks of it: insensible . . . I was a spirit, I tell you, remarkably fleet and dainty on my invisible feet—scarce touching the ground —whisking round with bright thoughts that looked into four fat heavy heads: empty caverns with ledgers stacked up against the windows to shut out the sun. Empty: barren: useless . . .

Counting was done with: the odds were reckoned. Which-ever way it went, I'd won. I was too quick for them. I'd time and enough to spare.

All in my golden moment I watched them swinging in the scales—and knew that one great weight would tip them up. This weight I had. Securely. I think I laughed. Some such sound was about. Then I cast in my weight.

"Gentlemen," I heard myself say. "The auction's over. I'll buy the lot!"

I cast in my weight. I emptied my bag on the table!

Chapter Nineteen

"LIKE musket-fire!" swore Mister Trumpet. "Like a volley of musket-fire!"

Heard it from the other end of the town: a sound to make a sieve of a man's heart! He'd hurried—run—fairly flown— for he'd a sudden dread, like a black pall on his sunshine—a

dread of what I'd do. There'd been a look in my eyes he'd not liked: a kind of madness—

By God! how the streets had fled under his feet! The boy's not right in the head, and he, Solomon Trumpet, had abandoned him! By God—

"Quick! Quick, good Mister Thompson! For pity's sake come with me! Here! Any hat'll do! Splendid! Fits like a glove! A proper gentleman! Only—come! Fly! I've a horrible feeling . . . that boy—Jack . . . We must save him!"

And then he heard it. Staggered as if he'd been shot!

"What's wrong, sir?" panted Mister Thompson. "What's amiss?"

"Like musket-fire! Did you hear it? Little coloured stones, Mister Thompson—falling, falling on a plain, deal table. Like musket-fire: and each one goes right through my heart. We're too late!"

This must have been when my flash of wisdom ran out: for, a moment later he burst into the hut dragging Mister Thompson after him—burst in with a cry of anguish as he saw my treasure piled on the table, glittering like mad.

"And not the stones alone," he said. Ibram Fared was nearly bursting out of his head at the sight of them. Also the two captains. And Sir Joseph was a deal whiter than his linen and drowned in sweat.

"And you! mad little fool, sat, it seemed, on air, like the small Arabian who'd rubbed his lamp and let loose a genie, not knowing, nor caring, what he'd done!"

"But I'd thought it all out, Mister Trumpet!" I protested, much hurt by his abuse.

"*Thought?*" jeered he. "I never saw a head more vacant nor a pair of eyes more glazed outside of Bedlam! Hearing nothing, seeing nothing, feeling nothing but your own lunatic ecstasies!"

Ecstasies? What ecstasies? When my flash of wisdom ran out, I never felt so sick in all my life. The clearness, the vision that had held the world at bay, broke—and all the pandemonium in the hut came tumbling in.

Mister Trumpet was shouting: "They're glass! Chipped glass! I know! I was a jeweller! Take no note of the boy! He's feverish! Don't rob him! It's glass, I say! Worthless! Worthless! Sentimental value only! Left him by his mother!"

"Very foolish young gentleman: sir! Very foolish gentleman. Too young to be rich: sir!"

"My honour, gentlemen . . ." Mister Fared fought to be heard. "My honour . . . untrue what you say! Honoured gentlemen—they're not glass . . . pardonable mistake . . . of course, of course—no offence . . . we do business . . . the young man has made an offer—I accept . . . I ACCEPT! Even if all be glass! Word is my bond! I have honour—still . . ."

And the two captains shouted and raged and roared at Mister Fared and Mister Trumpet and Mister Thompson and each other, for love of the little bright coloured things of which Nature herself thought so little as to make but a few of them.

"The auction's over, gentlemen. I've bought the lot!" I heard myself saying: and wondered wildly whether I'd said it before. And if I'd said it before, had anyone heard me? And if they'd heard, was it a bargain? And if it was a bargain, when would the settlement be?

"You got up and began to bang on the table," Mister Trumpet said, after. "Shouting you'd bought the lot. Some of the jewels jumped and fell on the floor. Then Mister Fared shrieked for silence. But none took any notice and Sir Joseph tried to put his great hoof on a diamond, pawing the ground like a horse, to bring it nearer. But Mister Fared saw him, and Lady Downs lost a pendant she nearly had.

"Then, somehow, we all fell out into the dusty sun. All save Mister Fared who'd contrived to cling inside and stuff his pockets with your jewels, Jack. Lord! how he rattled when he walked!"

But of this, I remember nothing. I must have fainted: for the next thing I recall was being among my purchases the slaves—my six hundred.

"All yours, young sir! All, all yours!" Mister Fared was quaking with riches and courtesy.

"What'll you do with 'em?" roared Sir Joseph. "Six hundred of them!"

What indeed was I to do with them? Sir Joseph had put his hairy finger on it. Six hundred—and all mine. Lord! Pestilentially, they seemed to crowd in on me—anguished, bleeding faces all . . .

"Five pound apiece, I'll give ye, lad! Five pound apiece, and keep the white man!" tempted Captain Farmer. (What a soft voice that hard man had!)

Five times six hundred? Three thousand pounds. A little fortune. In exchange for a million? Not such a fool, Jack! Not such a measly fool as that! To blazes, Captain Farmer! I want more for my million than three thousand sweaty pounds!

"That's right, young gentleman—that's the spirit! Let no man cheat you—"

"Sir! Young sir! Remember: three thousand pound in pocket better than nothing: sir!"

"Six pound ten apiece—and fourteen hundred guineas for the pygmy!" Now the Portuguese, smiling and edging up to me till I was forced back against Mister Trumpet.

"Damn you, Jack! What'll you do with them all? Answer me, Jack! Answer! Answer, before we all rot in this dreadful sun!"

For the sun was dreadful at that moment, glaring down like an angry eye. And the world was dreadful under it—full of greedy, cozening, once-white faces, thrusting out the six hundred mournful black . . .

What was in my mind? Nothing: save, it was hot; and the flies were as troublesome as the men: none would leave me in peace. My purposes were not theirs.

Where was he chained? Where was he waiting? Not far—down this lane of disaster . . .

"Sell! Sell, lad!"

The end of the lane! Thank God! No more of it! He never

came to meet me, smiling and open-armed, being still chained to his place. He stayed where he was, intent on his neighbour, the pygmy, who, after all, was a wonder, and rare.

But I'd done it! Found him! Saved him! Even bought him, lock, stock and barrel! Had to pay a million! Lumbered with six hundred extras! But *he* was preserved!

"Is this the one, young gentleman? Is this your heart's desire? Not the pygmy at all? Ah! I guessed he was dear to someone! Splendid, splendid! In good condition . . a trifle thin from worry, maybe? But he'll fatten . . . they always do! and the lash-marks will fade . . . they always do! Ibram Fared keeps faith! A bargain's made, struck, completed!

"Smiths! Come quick and free this friend for the young gentleman! You *do* desire him free, young gentleman?" (anxiously), "Or maybe you want him in chains? Can be done. Can separate him and keep him manacled. Patent device. Clever. Take him chained and decide at leisure: to free or not to free! See how he bites his lip! A little pleasure for your money . . . for your wealth's sake, take a little pleasure!"

I stood stock still, and stared. Bewildered. Amazed. Was this the man I'd come to save? Gone was the fish-like look. He gazed up at me, not grateful, not pleased: not anything but —angrily! Sharply, coldly, disbelievingly angry! That thankless lord was scowling! And when I'd given so much to save him!

"I've bought you," I muttered, suddenly sicker than ever. (I must have been mad! Mad! But in my flash of wisdom, all had seemed so right and clear—)

"Yes," said he, holding out his hands for his chains to be struck off. "And you were over-charged."

"I think so too," said I, remembering my lost pile of treasure and all it might have done for me.

"Poor boy . . . poor boy . . ." I heard Mister Thompson sigh: and Mister Trumpet's breath came and went like a furnace.

The chains were stretched over a stone, and before the hammer fell, he asked: "Are you sure you want me free, Jack? Think hard. Mister Fared, here, suggested a little pleasure from keeping me in abeyance. And why not, indeed?"

I shook my head and turned away while the hammer smote down six, seven times: until he was free.

"Will you have the others loaded aboard?" I heard his damned voice asking. "Or d'ye intend to sell again? If to sell, I ask a favour. Spare my friend Shem—the pygmy. That's all I ask of you. Spare him the shame of being sold."

(That's all, eh? That's all! No other trifle, like the sun for his ring finger—the moon for his fob?)

"Come, laddie: make up your mind. If to load, we must do so now," said Captain Farmer, brusquely. "If to sell, sell now."

"Make up your mind, Jack."

"What *was* in your mind to do with them, Jack? You must have some idea?"

Idea? Yes: maybe I did. In my flash of wisdom. There were no loose ends then. All was taken care of. But that flash was long since gone and I was left with the burnt-out wreckage of it. What was to be done? What had I meant to do? Set up as a farmer in the Indies with my strong six hundred? Sell them again? Take them back home with me? God knew!

"Cut your losses, laddie: sell!"

"Come, Jack! Sell and be done with it! Lose like a man and we'll all go home."

This was Mister Trumpet's advice. Then Mister Thompson, who'd been observing me narrowly and sadly through all the commotion of urging and tempting, plucked Mister Trumpet aside.

"Kiss the thousands goodbye! The young gentleman cannot see his way clear to sell. Pity tore such a hole in his pocket that a million fell through. Where in the world would he put a small three thousand? Sir! But comfort yourself, good Mister Trumpet: comfort yourself. Our friend is, maybe, a fool: but

not a small one. He is the largest fool it has ever been my
honour to know: sir!"

Mister Thompson's words dinned in my ears till I could
scarce hear myself shouting to Mister Fared and his smiths:

"Set them *all* free! Every last one! Let *them* go home, too!
Let's at least cheat the flies!"

Then I turned to Mister Trumpet and asked him—as I was
a pauper again—whether he'd pay my fare back home.

Then it was that the freed Lord Sheringham had the grace
to smile; and the grace to lay his hand on my shoulder: and I
had the grace to knock it off again.

The very last thing I wanted was his pity. Better the spiteful
rage of the captains, ("Mad little fool! Ought to be a law—
ought to be stopped—"): the contempt of Mister Fared and
Sir Joseph: the disappointment of Mister Trumpet, and the
deep black concern of Mister Thompson . . . Better all these
and more than the pity from him whom I'd saved.

Everyone seemed to melt away from me now, for, having
nothing more to say or give, I was no more than a bad taste
in their memories: the fool who'd put his foot through the
eggshell of their fortunes.

And for what? For Lord Sheringham's pity, six hundred
fleeting "Thank yous", and a paddock fast emptying of its
slaves.

Lord Sheringham stared at me curiously. Then he spoke to
the pygmy who'd not left his side.

"Shem: this is Jack, of whom I've told you. You and he have
much in common I fancy, having acted, at one time or another,
in a like way."

After this, which should have been my greatest moment,
but had somehow gone sour, we walked slowly and emptily
back to the waterfront: to Mister Thompson's for a suit for my
purchase, and to Captain Farmer for a passage back home.

Lord Sheringham and Mister Trumpet walked on ahead,
talking in low tones of the death of Mister Morris. Every now

and then, they would look back to see if I still followed—
though why they bothered was a mystery, as I'd nothing left
to be spendthrift with, save my life. Shem, the pygmy, whose
head came below my shoulder, walked silently at my side,
eyes downcast with his customary gravity. The others were all
gone: Mister Fared with the Portuguese captain—and Sir
Joseph at the heels of Captain Farmer.

In Mister Thompson's stuffy shop, ten pounds went a fair
way to making the great Judge a gentleman again: though, for
my part, I thought the money wildly spent. As much could
have been done with half: but his Lordship had an extravagant
streak in him, and chose as dear as he could. Poor Mister
Trumpet, who was paying (Lord Sheringham had improvi-
dently dropped *his* treasure in the forest when he was taken),
poor Mister Trumpet went outside to spare himself. Also, he
went to secure our passage on Captain Farmer's ship.

This cost him a good part of his two hundred guineas: but
he put a good face on it and tried to make out he'd struck a
shrewd bargain. (He always thought it dishonourable to be
cheated: disgraceful, almost.)

Then, by late afternoon, after a dinner of strange meat and
Madeira wine with Mister Thompson (a gift, thank the Lord!
else it would have cost a fortune!), we went aboard the *Lady
Jane*: a vessel somewhat larger than the *Charming Molly*,
having sixteen cannon polished as bright as Mister Morris
could have wished.

Lord Sheringham was a little put out that his friend Shem
had gone without great farewells: but I fancied he'd soon get
over the loss.

Mister Thompson was agreeable to the very last: as well
he might have been, having made considerable profits out of
our brief acquaintance—even to the last ten pounds for his
lordship's fancy clothes. (A gold topped cane he had to have!
As if plain wood wouldn't have supported him as well!) He
shook each of us by the hand—mine first and last—and said
it was a day he'd remember for all his life. "Holborn's Day",

he was going to call it—"Holborn's Day, the twenty-third of September. Each year I keep it as a holiday, and do no work. There! To remind me of your dear self: sir!"

By late afternoon, then, on that twenty-third of September, we went aboard the *Lady Jane*. And as we stepped over her side, it occurred to me to remind Lord Sheringham of something. So I did: and he turned and looked at me in hurt surprise—as if I'd stuck a knife in him.

"M'lord," I'd said. "This is the *second* time I've saved you. There's only one more to come."

Chapter Twenty

THE first day at sea: bright and calmish with a good following wind. If it stayed so, we should be at Weymouth by November.

Night came sharp and sudden in those waters, with the sun slipping like a sovereign into a quiet pocket. Then double watches were set at all points starboard and larboard, and two men stayed aloft.

Then I to bed alone, while Mister T. and Lord S. ("Mister Rogers" aboard: plain "Mister Rogers"), stayed up late in the great cabin, with Sir Joseph and Captain Farmer, drowsing over the sticky, sick-making Madeira wine.

Then Mister Trumpet and "Mister Rogers" would come back, talking loudly till they recollected that I might be sleeping. So they'd stumble into their bunks while I lay quiet, waiting for them to fall asleep and leave me to watch out the night while the *Lady Jane* sighed and creaked like a dowager in her stays.

At the end of the first week a squall sprang up so suddenly

there was not time to hoist storm canvas. Our foresail was rent right across and the sailmaker took two days to repair the damage, stitching and grunting and tugging the light-long hours.

"Come easy there! Ugh! D'ye see these hands? These braided fingers, lad? Remember 'em, so when ye sees a man with such horny mitts, so deep and shiny grooved about the forefinger, ye'll know his trade and honour him for it. Buy him a mug of ale and say, 'There's better things to stitch than shrouds and breeches, sir! And yours be the hands that stitch 'em! Here's to fine weather, sir, for all your salty days!' Ugh! Ugh! Come easy, there! Tight! Tight!"

During the day following the squall, we passed several snapped-off spars with their fractures still fresh: so a look-out was kept for more signs of a wreck. But none was seen, and it was surmised that the spars were all that remained of the too-light Portuguese—"gone down with all hands".

Mister Fared had been aboard—rich Mister Fared with all my jewels. Now he was with Mister Pobjoy and Mister Taplow, wafting the stones between them.

After nearly six weeks we touched on Lisbon where Captain Farmer and Sir Joseph sold their cargo of salt and silk for many casks of Port wine and Madeira, and "Mister Rogers", in an amiable mood, put it to me that, if nothing offered, I might come with him to London and make my home in his house. This he said hesitantly—and then recollected he'd some business to fix first which might take a few days. But, he assured me, he'd see I was well taken care of the while.

This, I presumed, was in exchange for having saved his life. I thought the bargain unjust. It seemed to me I was being swindled. And with the gentlest of smiles. Which vanished when I told him he'd best think of something better to discharge his obligation (which something he knew quite well), else wait till Providence provided the chance for us to be quit of one another for ever. Which chance, I hoped, would not be long delayed.

Three weeks later, upon a cold, Novemberish day, with the Channel mists dragging through the rigging and muffling up the masts, we reached St Peterport: and that's where the stranger came aboard.

Toward evening we sailed into the dark, very secret-seeming harbour and the old grey waters lapped and nudged the *Lady Jane's* deep timbers. Very cold it was on deck, and sombre in the cabins. Only Captain Farmer went ashore. He stayed about two hours and came back with a passenger for Weymouth: a tall muffled man who walked with a swinging lurch and skirted the mainmast as if it had been alive.

At first, I thought he was a melancholy madman, standing up there by the foremast, never moving: sometime blotted out by clots of fog, then growing solid again, still and strange as ever. He never spoke nor nodded nor waved to any living soul, but stared and stared across the dirty sea as if he was looking for a particular wave . . .

Then, suddenly, he turned and I saw he wore a brown patch that hid a ruined eye and part of a wound stretching clean down his face—from brow to jaw—which wound must have done for his sight. Also, upon the same side—his left—hung a sleeve, empty from the shoulder. His arm had been sheared off.

Presently, the weather grew better and the sun came out: though it was more like a painting of a sun—all light and no heat—while the wind was as cold as knives.

"D'ye ken yon grey ladies, laddie?" called out a Scots gunner, of a sudden. He pointed, and I saw, creeping out of the half-golden mists on our starboard bow, several tall grey rocks bearing a strange likeness to shuffling nuns, one nodding after another.

"How many d'ye ken?"

"Seven," said I, staring hard: for the last two were not much above water.

"Then ye may be thankful. If there'd been only five, it would ha' meant two had gone below to prepare our graves."

I must have looked disbelieving, because he wagged his

finger at me and said: "If there was five, we'd be done for. Believe me, laddie. Believe me."

Then a strange voice said: "It's a matter of angles and vision, son. If the last two rocks are hid, then the ship is on a line straight for the reef and will surely founder. For to be close enough to count them, is to be too close to haul off."

These were the first words I heard the one-armed stranger speak: and, certainly, his voice was more agreeable than his appearance. Yet there was something about it that seemed familiar . . .

For a long time this puzzled me; till I decided it was on account of his accent which resembled one or other of the *Charming Molly*'s crew. I could not remember which.

Once having heard him, and seen his single eye soften and twinkle, I thought of him quite differently and liked him for the way he talked with me, and told me things about the sea and weather. (Yes, he remembered the great storm some months back, with a cloud in the sky like a tiger. Some said there'd been earthquakes in London to match it.)

Every now and again, when I moved to catch his words better, he'd wince away from me. By this I knew his wound was still raw and the stump still tender.

How long since his calamity? Long enough to be mighty skilful with his one hand: yet not long enough to make up for his lost eye. Plain objects he had to skirt widely, and often seemed to see things toward his blind side that weren't there at all: while others he missed altogether . . .

By late afternoon it was certain we'd reach Weymouth by nightfall: for the following wind continued strong, and, under a rich spread of canvas, we made good speed.

Warmer and warmer grew the stranger as the hours to Weymouth shrank, and a "farewelling" air settled about all the *Lady Jane*.

He asked me what I did, where I lived, who I was travelling with, and whether I'd take a bite to eat with him when we went ashore.

"Ask your companions," he urged. "Ask them if they'll spare you for an hour or two."

"That I will, sir," said I, vastly flattered by the attention. "I'll ask directly."

For I'd just seen Mister Trumpet and "Mister Rogers" most opportunely on the half-deck for the first time that day.

"That's them over there—at the rail—d'you—" I broke off in sudden pain and astonishment—My wrist! He'd caught hold of my wrist in a grip that nearly broke it!

"What man is that?"

"My wrist, sir—my wrist—"

"What—man—is—that?"

"Which? Which man?"

"The little one. The grey-haired one—the one with the gold-handled cane."

"Mister Rogers. That's Mister Rogers."

He let go my wrist and strode clumsily forward to the bows of the *Lady Jane*. And there he remained, wrapped in an extraordinary silence. He never spoke to me or any other soul aboard again, and remained still as a rock, come fog, come dusk, come Weymouth itself. Then he and we and all the ship's company went ashore.

I asked Mister Trumpet if he'd ever seen the stranger before. "Never," said he. "Never in all his born days." But Mister Trumpet was so taken up in his coming life of ease and affluence that if the stranger had been his own brother he'd not have noticed.

I asked "Mister Rogers", and got no more than, "not to his certain knowledge . . . a mistake, maybe: impaired sight . . . took him for another . . . failing light plays tricks . . . overwrought. No . . no . . never seen him before—"

Then, at about eight o'clock on the foggy evening of November twenty-fifth, we nodded into Weymouth harbour. Ten minutes after that, we were ashore! Home in the dirty fog and stinking air, clattering once more on cobbles. (Lord!

they felt good! And once I'd run to leave 'em? Jack Holborn? Well, not quite the same Jack Holborn that went.)

Then I saw him again: tall and forbidding in the wreathing fog. His solitary eye was staring at "Mister Rogers". He turned on his heel and vanished into the busy night.

Chapter Twenty-one

WE found shelter for that night in the dingy North Star in Watergate Street, and there Mister Trumpet declared we must all take the morning coach to London.

"So we remain together?" said "Mister Rogers", somewhat surprised.

"Until London—until London. That's our centre. That's the heart of our world. That's where we all began: that's where we all must end."

"End?"

"Our acquaintance. Part. Separate. Disperse. You to London, 'Mister Rogers', to take up your life again: to patch up its holes, refurbish where it's grown shabby, restore where it's decayed. I to London on business—" He smiled, and I saw him drift momentarily into dreams of surprising old friends and astonishing old enemies: of dangling rich jewels before bulging eyes—of Solomon blowing his own Trumpet.

"Yes . . . on business. And Jack—"

"What of Jack?" (Not me that asked: but "Mister Rogers". Interested. Sharp. Concerned about a lad loose in London.)

"Jack to London because—"

"Because he's a London lad!" This was a laugh, and I half expected him to say again, "And I like a London lad!" but he didn't, and things were left as they were. I to London because I was a London lad. A fair enough reason. Every mouse to its hole: every scab to its wound: every corpse to its grave . . .

At half-past ten, we went up to bed: one room for the three of us. Though we were well enough dressed for the independent port of N—, we were pretty poor fish for Weymouth: not of much account even in the dingy North Star. How shabby even Mister Trumpet looked . . .

Mister Trumpet and "Mister Rogers" got off to sleep without more ado, but the grinding and banging of a church clock kept me awake.

Half-way through midnight, I left my bed and went to the window. The fog was cleared and the long street lay under the shaking moon.

Somehow, I'd known what I was going to see: yet when I did, it still gave me a violent shock.

Opposite, his one eye staring steadily up, was the mutilated stranger! For an instant, our looks met: mine astonished—his, malignantly triumphant. Then he turned and hurried away. He had discovered us.

I don't think it ever crossed my mind to wake my companions. Instead, I dressed rapidly and crept out into the cold, quiet street.

It seemed to me, that stranger and me had business together. We had a common interest. One "Mister Rogers".

He went swift and direct, with his swinging, lurching gait—unbalanced on account of his missing left arm. He never looked back and several times knocked against drunken men who staggered in his way. Two chairmen nearly did for him, crossing a square: danced this way and that—politely—irritably: then, laughing, let him by; and off he went, quick! quick! as if the Devil was at his clop-clopping heels.

I followed him to a square-built, modern house that stood in small neat grounds, hard by the waterfront. A pleasant, gentlemanly house, with good windows and a clean door.

I'd been expecting something different—something in the way of a reeking alehouse . . .

Yet what I heard through the opened window (for the bag-wigged old man who lived there smoked a long pipe that half choked the stranger, till, grumbling, he opened a window, cold as the night was) reeked high enough.

I heard a tale of sea-storm and wreck: and of a good ship, manned with charity and rigged with mercy, that sped to the aid of the sinking.

All this came, half-familiarly, as it were, while I crouched outside. Then the tale went on in the stranger's now calm, now shaking voice: coming nearer and nearer to the time I was born into it.

"Well for God's sake!" he cried again—exactly as I'd heard him shout it once before—(So that's why his voice had been so familiar!): and Taplow, Clarke, the Dutchman, frowsy Pobjoy, the terrible brothers Fox, and neat, cold Mister Morris himself came back to life! Only this was a life I'd never seen.

One by malevolent one they came slipping over the side— ("Amidships: the larboard side.")—of that first fine *Charming Molly*. And one by one the stranger described them—exactly— in the way of a man who has thought of nothing else thereafter.

"And then? And then?" asked the old man.

"Why, then they set to work."

I listened, freezing cold, while the stranger told on.

Pobjoy, Hughes, Clarke, Suckling and the rest were wicked men, I knew; but I'd lived so long among them, and they'd lived so easy in my mind, that I'd come hever to think worse of them as lazy, oathful scavengers: fellows who sometime cursed and laughed and spat and snored and scratched themselves: and loved the sun, save when it grew too hot.

Now I saw them again as they set about murdering the crew and seven passengers that day aboard the *Charming Molly*. Like frantic, sweating, wild beasts, they were, as the hacking and slicing and stabbing and chopping told on their wearying arms.

"And this—this 'Mister Rogers', d'ye say, was in command of 'em? He was in the thick of it?"

"He came aboard when the worst was over. It was he who shot down the four surviving female passengers. Lined them up on the larboard rail and, from six paces distant, put a ball in each of their heads."

"And you, friend—you were—?"

"By the forecastle. Lying for dead. Lying as if I was sleeping—" He paused, then continued: "My head in the crook of an arm. It was still warm, that arm. It had once been mine. Yet . . the fingers looked . . . looked strange—"

"And ye'll swear this 'Rogers' was the self-same man? No chance of a wounded man's fancy? No chance of error?"

"None."

"Then the warrants shall be sworn. The North Star, d'ye say? Watergate Street? The warrants! The warrants! And, look ye, sir—guard yourself well. You're the only witness. Fall, or trip, or perish by cold and he goes free. Guard yourself, man. Especially against sharp steel."

Chapter Twenty-two

THE old man left the room.

Already I'd got to my feet to be off to warn—for the precious third saving—when, with his back to me, the stranger called out:

"One warrant, sir! Only one warrant! It'll be enough!"

And the old Justice came stumbling back.

"What was that, friend. One warrant? But ye told me at the beginning there were three of them. Three, ye said: Mister Rogers, another man—and a boy."

"Yes—yes—I know. But there's nothing against the other two. Shipboard acquaintances of Rogers. No more than that. I know it."

"But ye said the boy seemed much attached to Rogers—What if he turns out to be Rogers' son, eh? Cut off the old head and the young one grows twice as strong. Like roses!"

"He wasn't the son. No resemblance. Chalk and cheese."

"Many's the cheese I've tasted ye'd be hard put to tell from chalk! I'd best make out all three warrants to be safe, eh?"

"No! No! I'll not be witness against the others!" The stranger was grown passionate. Did he know I was listening? Did he want me to hear? Did he want to delay me on my way to warn Mister Rogers? A clever, desperate man. He went on: "The boy knew nothing of Rogers. Nothing! If he'd an inkling, a shred of suspicion of what that man was like, he'd not have sailed the same sea!"—His voice grew louder: "How could a lad, scarce fourteen, know of such things—and continue with them! Of course he liked Rogers! The fellow is very personable! The lad's honest—and looks through honest eyes! A fault, d'you say? Maybe: but not punishable.

"Why, sir, d'you think that such a lad—who'll make a man to be proud of some day, if you and me and the law let him—if he knew what wrinkled Rogers had done, d'you think he'd stand by and let him do it again and again?

"D'you think he'd suffer such sins to fester on his conscience? And no matter *what* the reward for silence! God, man, the lad I met and talked with would have been at your door before me!"

He stopped, breathing hard—in the way of a man who has expended much energy in a great effort: and awaits the result.

The Justice grunted: "Boys' natures are queer animals, friend. Bats' wings and flies' eyes are simple beside 'em. This lad may be tied to your Rogers by stronger bonds than you know of."

"Then he'll break them!"

After this, I heard the old man shuffle to the door, mumbling as he went: "By the Lord Harry, that lad's lucky ye lost the eye that might have seen through him! By the Lord Harry, that eye'll cost ye dearer yet! If that same lad could hear ye now, I'll wager he'd be laughing his cunning little head off!"

I got to the North Star about ten minutes ahead of the constables. Mister Trumpet and "Mister Rogers" were sleeping very soundly. Mister Trumpet, as usual, slept with his hand under his pillow, clutching the White Lady. His bed was nearest the door.

"Mister Trumpet," I whispered. He stirred and moved his hand. I snatched the stone—and fled.

He caught me up about a hundred yards down Watergate Street, where it turned into a narrow lane. Grabbed hold of my shoulder fiercely: called me: "Lunatic! Madman! Idiot!" But he never called me "thief"—even though he was wild with fury. He never quite forgot himself.

I handed back the White Lady (a cold stone, no matter how much it was clutched), and he looked at it bitterly, as if blaming it for all the world's wickedness, as if the fires it struck in men's hearts were but reflections of its own icy glitter.

He put it away and said: "Come back to bed quietly. Maybe he's not roused. No need for him to know of it."—He never accused me: never blamed me. "If he's awake, say you felt sick . . . went out for air . . . and I came too. Say no more than that."

We'd begun to walk back—slowly as I could make him. But even before we'd started, it was too late. The constables were knocking on the door. Mister Trumpet made to hurry—but I dragged him back. That's how he guessed that I knew.

He was dazed with sleep when they took him; faintly protesting: "I'll go with ye quietly . . . no need for force . . . no need . . ."

I heard them ask of his companions: but all they got was: "Friends of passage . . . no more . . . don't know 'em . . . I'm alone . . . quite alone . . . alone . . . ."

Then they bundled him off down the street in a jerking knot of shadows, which kept splitting and joining again as he tried to walk alone and with dignity—and they wouldn't let him ... He was to be dragged off to prison: and dragged off he was.

Mister Trumpet and me were left alone in that cold, cold street: very quiet and empty. Mister Trumpet never looked at me, nor never spoke: but went slowly back into the North Star where the startled landlord and his sad wife watched us up the stairs then locked and bolted the door.

Came morning and Mister Trumpet brought himself to ask me: "Why did you do it, Jack? What possessed you? It wasn't for money, was it? For God's sake, say it wasn't for money!"

I shook my head: tried to explain. Betrayal by omission was as bad as by commission. By failing to warn "Mister Rogers", I'd secured for certain the arrest of Lord Sheringham.

Mister Trumpet looked hard, trying to understand me, ("Boys' natures are queer animals—"), maybe to forgive me for what I'd done. I don't think he succeeded. But the effort counted for much.

By not turning from me then—for he'd much to lose himself if I was a natural born traitor—(he being on the wrong side of the law, too soon home from transportation), by not turning from me, he showed great compassion and real gentlemanliness of a rare sort.

"What is it in you, Jack? Twice, to my knowledge, you've saved him—" Mister Trumpet went on in puzzlement. "Once, at the risk of your life. A second time to the ruin of your pocket. And now—when nothing was at stake—no risk to life or limb—you chance your good name to finish him off. What's your philosophy of it all, Jack? Health and wealth you're prepared to sacrifice. What's the third thing you can't give up? D'you know your unhappy self?"

The coach for London was to leave at eleven. I wondered if

Mister Trumpet would try to see him before we went. (For we were going to London regardless of disaster.) But he sat about in the North Star's parlour, staring out of the window and glancing, from time to time, at the clock. Maybe he was wondering if I'd go? He looked glum enough to be wondering such a thing. But I'd neither the will nor the courage to face that man in his last extremity—to which I'd brought him. Besides, he'd only have thought I'd come to plead for my secret. And that I'd put behind me now.

"I thought you was bound to him, Jack," said Mister Trumpet, at length.

I shook my head.

"Will you see him before we go, Jack?"

"No."

"Maybe it's as well. Cut adrift—and cut clean, eh?"

"Will you go, Mister Trumpet?"

He shook his head. No sense in his going. What could be done?

Though he never said it, it was plain he wouldn't go because he didn't want to be asked who had been the traitor . . . He preferred that Lord Sheringham, our lost companion, should not be distressed by an unnecessary truth.

Gloomily, I felt that, though Mister Trumpet still continued with me, it was now because of pity: all liking was gone.

At about quarter past ten, a frowsy-looking customer came into the North Star. (This was the man who brought the first note.)

He looked about him. "Master Jack Holborn?"

I nodded—half guessing.

"What's it worth to you?" He held out the folded paper. For a moment, I thought it was my secret, generously given. Coals of fire. In which event, the paper was worth—

"—A mug of ale," said Mister Trumpet.

The messenger got the best of the bargain. I got only three words. *Come to me. S.*

"Any answer, Master Holborn?"

"None. No answer."

The London coach left Weymouth sharp on eleven: and until that very minute, I think Mister Trumpet expected—even wanted me to go off in answer to the note. He kept looking up at the church clock, and telling me how much time there was in hand. He kept pacing the yard, and telling me . . . Then, when it was plain I'd not go, he frowned as if he'd come upon darknesses in human nature he'd not dreamed of.

It was a full five minutes after we'd moved off that I began to have regrets. For I imagined it was possible, in this last extremity, he—the man in gaol—had reached a point when evil would do him no more good: and kindness could do him no harm. I conceived he might be desirous of making me a present—and a confession.

This maggot of hope gnawed at me all the way to Dorchester. There was nothing else to think about: nothing to look at for distraction. It was raining hard and the coach windows were streaming with restless rivers of tears.

One word from Mister Trumpet then, and I'd have gone back—even in that dismal rain. But no such word came. He'd made friends in the coach and spared me scarcely a look.

I began to think of borrowing a guinea from him to go back with. For what had I to hope for from London? Hope, such as it was, lay in Weymouth gaol. A tormenting hope I'd thought was dead.

At the inn at Blandford I'd resolved to trouble Mister Trumpet for that guinea. It was a worldly inn—and Mister Trumpet was a worldly man. Half a dozen travellers were in the parlour and Mister Trumpet was explaining to the landlord how to mull wine.

The landlord would have answered him—looked eager to—but it was then that the soaking, many-caped gentleman came in and demanded instant serving.

Very searchingly, he looked about the room, then half-smiled and fixed on Mister Trumpet. He came over and asked softly: "Are you the husband of the White Lady: and have you a friend in trouble?"

Mister Trumpet frowned, and nodded: and the second note was produced. This time it was not to me.

Mister Trumpet read it: twice: then put it away. He would not show it to me. I decided to put off borrowing the guinea till I knew what was in it.

But this was delayed until we reached Salisbury, where we spent the night. He gave it to me after supper—without a word—handed it to me like a last course.

This time more was written.

Seventeen Dover Street. London. But for God's sake, don't take the boy. S.

I decided, finally, not to borrow the guinea.

Chapter Twenty-three

WE reached London in the rain and dark of the twenty-eighth of November: the George Inn at Southwark—not far from Holborn. I'd come nearly full circle. From there we went direct to Dover Street, and my good friend Mister Trumpet paid his first call on Number Seventeen.

The shock nearly killed him. When he got back he was white as the ghost he thought he'd seen: soaked to the skin from standing stock-still in the pouring rain . . . .

My good friend, Mister Trumpet . . . These were his days and he rose to them like an eagle . . .

It had been agreed that I should wait in the warm in a near-by inn. Which I did, freezing with expectation before the idle fire for close upon half an hour. Then he came back and told me what he'd seen in the window of Number Seventeen, and the whole world was forgot. The poor fire, the browned walls and dusky ceiling—even London itself—all seemed to dissolve away and I was back upon the *Charming Molly* in those first few hopeful days.

He said he'd seen a man from the *Charming Molly*: a man with a country complexion, close-cut grey hair, and curious fish-like eyes.

"But he's in Weymouth Gaol!"

"But he's in Dover Street!"

"You're mad, Mister Trumpet!"

"So's Nature, Jack Holborn: for she's made two of them!"

"What d'you mean?"

"Twins, Jack Holborn! There are twins, my lad! Two brothers with the same face!"

"My God, Mister Trumpet! My God!"

"Yes, indeed, Jack—there's not much else left to trust in, is there, old son? Unless the Devil is His twin—"

He paused, and then went on half to himself, "The man in Weymouth is the Judge—for he knew me. The man in Dover Street is the other: and he knows you, Jack. He knows you from those first days aboard the *Molly* before I came. That's the reason for the note! Of course it is! 'For God's sake' indeed don't take the boy!"

He hunched his shoulders and frowned—then began to recall some things he heard long ago: that Lord Sheringham had a property on the South Coast: that Lord Sheringham went there rarely on account of some family uneasiness: that it had been vaguely and darkly rumoured that there was a brother ... very like ... but not so honourable ...

God knew what hateful shame and guilt the existence of so foul a twin must have brought upon the Judge! The constant dread that that man came sometimes ashore and was mistook for him! The thought that all his own honour and goodness could be worn like a borrowed suit and most maliciously stained! And he must have had cause for such fears. Maybe not so much for himself but for those who were deceived and so ruined and damned by what they took for virtue. For there's no evil so abominable as that which is took for goodness.

"Then—did he mean to kill his own brother?"

"I think, maybe, he was driven to it—to do it with his own hands, Jack. For he could never have brought himself to have him publicly hanged. But when his chance came—"

"—the ambush?"

"The ambush. A double betrayal, I fancy. Your Captain was ready for it. God above! what a meeting it must have been—there in the dark on the beach! So they fought—and the wirier, wickeder won and left the other, luckless, three parts dead Lord Sheringham to be dragged back aboard the *Charming Molly* by deceived Mister Morris. There must have been a pleasant smile on his face when he watched that damaging corpse being so considerately removed!"

A sullen pot-boy elbowed by and humped a new log onto the dying fire. It hissed and shook and sent up a storm of sparks that perished in the black hole of the chimney. Then the fresh wood began to catch, little tongues nervously tasting it—more and more—till at last it became a ghost of itself behind a bright yellow veil of flame.

And all the while I was thinking of that three-quarters corpse (lovingly tended by mistake) that failed to die as had been confidently hoped. It lived—and woke. And what a wakening it must have been!

The terror and loneliness of it! How he must have sought for a friend—even such a one as I. And I'd met him with equivocal mysteries: saved his life—then demanded unknown payment! Seemed honest—yet looked and dreamed and spoke in mad riddles.

What kind of a world had he come into? When I'd seemed to be near him, I'd turned weirdly away . . .

The coming of Mister Trumpet: the agony of recognition: deception on deception—further and further into the mire till there seemed no turning back: pushed and succoured by loyal Mister Morris—bitterly mistaken loyalty, that! Falsest of false pretences! Mister Morris: such a man! Burdened with black honour . . . Yet did he guess? Towards the end, did he half understand?

"But why in Heaven's name did he never speak out, Mister Trumpet? Afterward, I mean—"

"Maybe he never quite trusted us?"

"Even to the end? Yes—I suppose it must have been so—but now—he'll be hanged! What's to be done? What *can* be done?"

"Everything! And at once! We've a debt to repay. To Lord Sheringham and ourselves. For we sent him out as a scapegoat, loaded with every sin in sight. And why? Because he wore a convenient face. I think, maybe, Mister Morris alone took the trouble to look deeper. And you know what it did to him."

"I think Mister Pobjoy sensed it too."

"And Taplow and the rest—for the storm drove them uncannily mad . . ."

"Mister Pobjoy said there'd be nothing between him and the sky if the Captain went . . ."

"Let's begone, Jack—and pray to God we're in time!"

Mister Trumpet was entirely transformed. He seemed to burn with the same forest-fever that drove him wild for the White Lady. Only now it was allied to a cold, almost ferocious calculation, the formidable power of which swept aside all "but"s and "maybe"s.

That very night he went in search of ends and threads he'd cut two years before: acquaintances . . . gentry who sailed upon the windy side of the Law. But in two years addresses can change. His best hope—who'd lived in Paternoster Row, was removed some fifty yards off, to a more permanent place in St Margaret's Churchyard . . .

So he knocked up another—a seedy attorney who'd sold his soul so often that he was like a spiritual circulating library with it. Mister Trumpet might have parted with less than the fifty guineas he did and got as much devotion.

"I want a certain Captain Rogers transferred at once from Weymouth Gaol to stand his trial at Old Bailey before Lord Sheringham. Can it be done?"

The attorney—unsurprised—thought awhile. He knew someone—who knew someone else—who was acquainted with another who knew a certain clerk with a wide net of interests . . . Yes, it was possible: for in such ways the whole world's acquainted . . .

Off we went with another address. Ten guineas—then to some two or three others, sometimes, even, led deviously back to next door to the one before the last. Having run out of guineas, Mister Trumpet dealt henceforward in tiny gems till at last he'd secured an extraordinary net of co-operation. Everything was subtly secured—woven shrewdly together— so actions, seeming independent, functioned to one end. Nothing depended on one man: save on the man who sat in Dover Street. To him led all the bought threads. His seal and approval were needed. Was it possible? Could one purchase such an one as even the false Lord Sheringham? "Every man has his price," Mister Trumpet was assured—"even him. But what that price is, we leave to you to discover and meet."

At nine o'clock on the morning of the twenty-ninth of November, Mister Trumpet—on strong recommendation— went to Dover Street. An hour later, he came palely out. With what was required. How had he done it?

"He had his price, Jack."

"What was it, Mister Trumpet?"

"Only a diamond."

"Which one, sir?"

"What else but the White Lady, eh? Believe me, Jack— it was a real marriage between 'em!"

Mister Trumpet had sacrificed his heart's desire. I've said these were his great days—and this, I think, was almost the greatest.

On December the fifth, we learned that an alteration had taken place in the Old Bailey list. A certain Captain Rogers was to be tried before Lord Sheringham on December seven. At last the clouds were gone and the end lay clear in sight. Even though, from force of habit, I supposed, I fancied a small hump somewhere on the horizon . . .

Chapter Twenty-four

FRIDAY, December seven: an oppressive, warmish day provoking easy sweat.

"Jack," said Mister Trumpet to me in our lodgings. "You smell, old son."

"It's the weather!" said I, indignantly.

"No: it's you."

"What do I smell of then?"

"Oh, of doubts and dreads, and little panics that all will go wrong—"

"Then you've a long sharp nose!"

"Go upstairs and put some of my pomatum on your hair. Kill two birds with one stone."

I shrugged my shoulders and went. So my hair was like a bird's nest? Much I cared! The pomatum stank. When I came back, so did I: of it. Mister Trumpet nodded. Both birds were dead. And smelled it.

A man who pushed past us as we went into the Old Bailey, sniffed, looked back, and grinned: "Whiffs like His Lordship's posy, don't he!"

We got pew-seats at the back of the court from where we could peer up to the tremendous, dark empty Bench about

L

which attorneys, clerks and ushers buzzed and fizzed and crackled briefs till they'd be put a stop to.

Huge confusion. A lawyer's clerk, half-running, nearly on his knees, scuttled by, plucked my sleeve, asked if I'd earn a guinea. A witness had defaulted. I'd do. Easy—easy as falling off a bench.

I shook him off and he went like a crab down the aisle: found a seedy-looking man who'd oblige: led him off across the well of the court, deep in talk—the new witness wisely nodding. Most likely made his living so.

I wondered whose witness had defaulted. Not ours. That grim, mutilated man would have risen from his grave, if need be, to point his finger at the dock.

Then I realized ours wasn't the only affair of the day. Many must have been waiting. When was it to be, the trial of Captain Rogers? Not long to wait.

Then, quite suddenly, all the bustling and dartings to and fro, stopped. He was coming. Who? His blessed Lordship. The Judge: Lord Sheringham.

"Or his twin brother."

A gentleman in front, with ears too big for his wig, turned and rested his chin on our pew-top.

"Ha—ha! Very witty! Bright lad! Bright lad!"

"Be quiet, you damned little fool, Jack!" swore Mister Trumpet, and, as the court rose in respect, dragged me down so we were crouched behind the big-eared old elephant who'd thought so well of the law.

After which we sat and dared not look up to the Bench for more than one fierce glimpse.

"Good God! Mister Trumpet—he looks so different in his wig! The likeness'll never be seen! We're done for, I tell you!"

"Then go whip it off!"

"What? His wig? Now?"

"Then be quiet!"

He had me. Thenceforth I kept my dismay to myself. Yet

it was horribly true. A great, full-bottomed wig changes a man out of all recognition. His face sits in the middle quite dwarfed by it.

"Put up William Wild."

The day's work was begun. Nothing now could stop it.

I sat, staring down at the dusty floor and Mister Trumpet's hand, set like a claw on his rigid knee. Irresistibly, memories came into my mind: memories of the dark night in which I boarded the *Charming Molly* at Bristol. Memories of . . .

"There's none I like better than a London lad! Sharp: keen: to the point!"

Lord! how it took me back! His voice—so well-remembered-broke in. Was it still for William Wild? No: another wretch being eased out of his life. What was it all about? God knew!

The attorneys had been droning on: witnesses witnessing: accuseds swearing . . . Swearing what? That black was white. That men's eyes deceived them. That this man who saw them was mistook: that they were elsewhere—a dozen miles away at the vital time. That it was another man entirely—of similar features . . . very like . . . very like . . . A double that did the deed in question. The world seemed full of doubles that morning.

"A double! D'ye believe it, gentlemen of the jury? If ye do, ye'll believe anything! A double! What—*two* such ill-favoured rogues? A double! Ah, we all know such doubles, eh?"

He jibed and chuckled on: drawing nooses in the flattered jury's ears. And all in his sunshine voice.

"A gardener—a Christmas gardener—all for hanging bad fruit on the Tree!"

"Well said, lad! Very witty!" Our fat friend in front shook as he guffawed: and we bent low out of a diamond hard look from the Bench. Had he seen us? "For God's sake, Jack—keep silent!"

Why was our affair so long in coming? Why all the talk of doubles? Time and again . . . Was he haunted by the thought? Did he suspect? Was he preparing himself, us and the court for what was to come?

Then, at last, came the sound I'd been waiting for—
"Put up Captain Rogers."
Put him up . . . right up . . . well up . . .' 'For this is indeed a put-up job!"
"There's a bright fellow you've got there!"
"Put up Captain Rogers."
Pleasantly from the Bench: "*Captain* Rogers? Has he no christian name? Or maybe he's no Christian? Or is 'Captain' his christian name? Not very Christian: for before God we're all privates, eh?"
He laughed—and led the way for laughter. The attorneys laughed: the ushers guffawed: likewise the clerks and the jury. Merry men.
Our moment: I'd have given ten million pound to've been a mile away and known nothing till all was over! The tension in me and Mister Trumpet was terrible. I heard him breathing very raspingly: and my heart nearly broke open my ribs. Why hadn't he come? What was gone wrong?
Then the laughter thinned and faded—almost abruptly— ending on a single fool's cackle left in the air like he'd laid an egg and was ashamed of it.
I dared not look—neither to the Judge nor to the dock. But he was there: Captain Rogers. The Judge was gone white. Deathly.
"He's ill!" muttered someone. "A seizure!" Came a curious loud crack. This was his quill snapping between thumb and forefinger. (It takes a deal of strength to do that: considerable strength!)
At last, he spoke: harsh, strained words, dragged from a frozen brain . . . all he could do . . . all he could say . . . What a deadly moment for him! His heart must have gone to ice. But he struck back.
"I—cannot—try—this—man. He is known to me . . . has

been . . . for some time . . . I cannot try him. Another court. I cannot try this man . . ."

The air was gone hot, still, breathless. Men were half standing, craning forward: the fat man in front was grown to a mountain. I could see nothing. What were the guards doing? Standing back dumbfounded? And the ushers and the attorneys? A man coughed. Maybe the clerk choking on the unread indictment?

"I—cannot—try—this—man."

Mister Trumpet was gone from my side! I felt him slip away: heard him stumble over feet and knees towards the aisle. Angry whispers pursued him like a swarm of bees. Then he was hurrying down to the well of the court, his feet chattering on the boards. What now?

A third time, the voice from the Bench—maybe brought on by the sight of racing Mister Trumpet, and a sudden understanding of the plot.

"I cannot try this man."

"Why not? Why not?"

Mister Trumpet was begun. A violent muttering sprang up and began to blow across the court. "Who's that? . . . who is he . . . an attorney? . . . What's he doing? . . . He's mad! What a morning!"

"WHY NOT?"

"Because—"

"— He is my brother!"

Confusion! The same voice—yet it moved fifteen feet in mid-sentence. Who'd spoken? The Judge? The prisoner? Both. Each. With the addition of voice, the likeness between the two became marvellous—incredible. Eyes swung from one to the other—vainly seeking a difference, however slight—to mark one from the other. No such difference was found. The guards were struck powerless—unable to obey the man on the Bench. It would have been impossible to've hauled away his double. It would have seemed like molesting the great Judge

himself. Unable—or unwilling? Such vast excitement was not to be missed. Such a morning was to be noted, examined, marked in every particular for a tale to be remembered and told for ever . . .

"He is indeed my brother."

The voice was from the Bench. It went on, brokenly and sorrowfully, heaping such infamy on the head of "Captain Rogers" that it could only have been a portrait of himself. As if ashamed, he told the fascinated world that his brother *was—himself*!

The shadow on the horizon! It sprang on my hopes like a tiger! For where was the proof the prisoner was the Judge, and that the Judge, in all justice, should have been the prisoner? Where—*where*, Mister Trumpet. *This* was the something that had been overlooked!

Good God! Mister Trumpet, but you've undone us by this one damned oversight! Good God! Mister Trumpet, can you blame the world for not turning itself upside down? Why should the Judge be in the dock? What reason?

"Good God! but what's the fellow saying? What's he getting at? Where's he leading? All of us to Bedlam—or himself to Tyburn?"

Brazen Mister Trumpet was accusing the Judge of being false. Claiming that "Captain Rogers" was Lord Sheringham. Ushers came forward to stop him—to tear him away, when:

"Let him speak!" came the Judge's voice. From the dock. Some men began to laugh; nervously, incredulously. The situation was wild. Unnatural. And, if Nature had suspended her laws, men must suspend theirs. This was reasonable . . .

"Proof of identity! Proof! Proof!"

"Mister Gracechurch! Ye're a wise, learned counsel. Steeped in the law. Headed for the Bench. Tell this impudent fellow who I am and have done! Speak up, Mister Gracechurch!"

Mister Gracechurch, sleek, ambitious lawyer, renowned for

shrewd opinion and advantageous decision, looked up, looked down, fumbled among limp scrolls and a great book: stuttered, stammered, begged pardon and oozed out:

"Why, you're Lord Sheringham, m'lord!"

Then the prisoner demanded: "And who am I, Mister Gracechurch? Come, sir! Counsel's opinion: a point of law—speak up, Mister Gracechurch!"

Mister Gracechurch, red and white by turns, wishing himself asleep and in his bed—out of the nightmare—was struck by a ghastly thought. If the Judge was indeed in the dock by some mad mischance, where would *his* next stop be if he opined against him? The ladder of success seemed to have a rung missing.

"God knows who you are!" gave Mister Gracechurch as his opinion, at length: and added (disastrously, from habit of sight): "M'lord!"

A shrewd judgement. No gainsaying it. But Mister Gracechurch was wrecked by it: foundered: smashed in pieces. The Judge stared down at him with a strained and dreadful smile. No more would his opinion be sought. On the great ladder he'd missed his footing—and was done.

"Call Thomas Furnish!"

Who was Tom Furnish? Who wanted him? What business had he in all this? Furnish? Furnishings and hangings indeed! Who was due to be hanged? Mister Gracechurch had said God knew: and Mister Gracechurch was—or had been—a wise counsel. God knew who was going to die.

What if we'd been wrong then—and the Judge was the Judge and we'd been taken in? Impossible! Yet where was our proof—even to ourselves? There was none. None at all—else surely it would have been forthcoming. Of a sudden, I understood we were two against, not one evil man, but the whole world! And with nothing but our own believing for support. Had we been taken in? What a bitter twist to a fantastic tale that would have been!

"Is your name Thomas Furnish?"

It was the mutilated stranger! I'd never thought of him bearing a name! He came to the witness box.

"Which man did you see board the *Charming Molly?*" He pointed—to the dock. The Judge smiled. Mister Trumpet cried out: "Look to the Bench, man! Could it not have been—him?"

Tom Furnish looked, drew in his breath, wondered, hesitated: "Fantastic . . . truly so . . . hard to say . . . robes and wig . . . the man in the dock was more likely . . . but . . . but . . ."

"Can you swear—one way or the other?"

Honest man that he was, he could not swear. Was dismissed: nothing achieved. A thin hope gone. There'd been a chance that mutilated Tom Furnish might have seen the devil in one pair of eyes—and a good man in the other. But he'd only one eye himself: not enough to sort out so subtle a thing. So the faint hope went with him. The great fat fellow in front turned his enormous face on me:

"Your friend's played fast and loose—and lost! Bad luck—bad luck, eh?"

With a shock, I realised I could see *his* face twice over and understood I must have been sick, distempered with the heat and excitement: some pressure of intense air interfering with my brain . . . maybe through my ears which sang like a fiery choir . . .

"Jack Holborn! Jack Holborn! Come forward!" Mister Trumpet's voice: oh! the trumpeting of it! And the echoes—"Who's he? Who's Jack Holborn? What next? Another witness? Jack! Jack! Show yourself!"

They gave me a push and a shove, and maybe a kick—I can't remember for sure—but the way along the row and down the gaping, leggy aisle was damnably long so it was an eternity before I fell, like a loose tooth into the open mouth of the court.

"A boy! A lad! Look at him! Half out of his wits with terror!"

I saw Mister Trumpet's hand—took it, and went to the witness box. I think someone tried to stop me. I can't be sure. Perhaps it was my own feet . . .

"Which is the man you first saw aboard the *Charming Molly*?"

I looked—and saw Lord Sheringham in the dock: and Lord Sheringham on the Bench. Again the fear came over me of being mistook—of myself against the world. Neither spoke: neither smiled. Which one was which?

Now I like to think I saw something about one which was not so with the other. Now I like to think that. Else why did I point to the man on the Bench and hear myself stammer out: "It was him! He was the man!"

But upon the rest of my testimony, I'm none too sure. A great roar seemed to come up from the body of the court and sweep me away with it.

Questions I answered in that enormous storm—I scarce knew what they were. Questions from Mister Trumpet: calm, remorseless, like hammer-blows shaking me back into the world. Questions from the Bench: questions from the dock. Questions . . . questions . . . even from a clerk—(the Lord knows what he asked: likewise, the Lord knows what I answered).

"So he was the man who made you that promise?"

"Yes: he was the man."

No more can I remember who asked what that promise was: whether Mister Trumpet, the Judge—or the prisoner. Or maybe it was a voice in my distracted head to which I made answer aloud.

I told the court, my friends and the world, in exact terms, of the promise that, like a good following wind, had driven me with little ceasing since I'd heard of it. My secret, my deep, deep secret was out. It made a vast impression. Like treasured furniture, so splendid when confined in a home, but so pitiful when moved out into the street. So shabby and small.

"What? He hoped for that? Lord! what a fool!"

As I've said, it made a vast impression. On whom? Mister Trumpet? He looked as though he was sorry for me. Certainly I saw no other face that looked aught but entertained and astonished that it should matter to such an one as I who and what I was.

So I'd cast my weight into the scales—and it was of no effect: neither upon Lord Sheringham in the dock, nor upon Lord Sheringham on the Bench.

The Judge looked down on me and shook his head. What was all this to him? Nothing. Mister Trumpet beckoned me off. No more was to be achieved. I'd served my turn. Now was the time for ending. I heard the Judge say: "Enough—enough! Take them away." He had won.

The guards were moving, the court settling, when Mister Trumpet swung round and returned for the last attack.

Extraordinary man! Up to the witness box he mounted like one climbs a mainmast to the crosstrees: a thing I never saw him do in all his life—yet Mister Trumpet was very sailorlike in all things not connected with the sea. Then he grasped at two wooden posts like for support in a gale and leaned out on the court.

All unbidden, at the top of his loud voice, he swore to tell the truth. This was in the teeth of the now enraged Judge and his suddenly willing helpers who were ready and eager to drag Mister Trumpet down.

But with eloquent flailing arms—which made him hard to approach—and steady countenance, he laid before the court the tale of his visit to Number Seventeen Dover Street. He told how he'd bribed the man on the Bench to bring about— albeit, unwittingly—this astonishing morning.

The White Lady. He spoke of it—and the court was filled with eerie, glittering dreams. If there was a man present that morning who'd never heard of the great diamond, ten neighbours promptly told him at top speed: so none had cause to be ignorant.

The White Lady! Her name was on all lips. It was like being back in the forest when Mister Morris was alive and the wicked whispers were all about us.

"The White Lady? You must be mad! What should I know of such unlucky trash?"

"You deny it?"

"Most certainly I do!"

"You deny my visit to you?"

"Likewise—likewise—"

"You deny having seen me before?"

"I deny it. Thank God I've never seen you before!"

"You are lying!"

"You are insane!"

"Again I'll ask: have you seen me before?"

"Never."

"Then you've forgot. In scarce eight days you've forgot. So faulty a memory makes a bad judge: a false judge: a judge to be tried—and found wanting."

"I do not forget: nor will I forget: nor will you forget this dangerous morning. Never will you forget it."

"Because you've forgot me?"

"Listen, fellow: if I'd seen ye but once—twenty years ago— I'd remember. Not because of your distinction of countenance, but because of my distinction of memory. It would be as impossible for me to forget as for this exceeding wicked plot to succeed. D'ye understand? Ye've failed! Failed!"

At this, Mister Trumpet flung wide his arms in a very final gesture—and turned to the dock.

"Lord Sheringham."

"Yes—?" They answered together: but Mister Trumpet was not distracted. "If the man on the Bench had been who he claims to be, what should he have answered?"

"Silence! Silence! I order you to be silent!"

"Have done! Damn you—have done!" Lord Sheringham's voice cut like a whip—then he replied to Mister Trumpet:

"He should have answered that he *had* seen you before, Mister Solomon Trumpet."

"Where—and when?"

"Have you considered this? Are you certain? This is a great sacrifice."

"In a great cause, m'lord."

"Maybe—maybe—" he paused. "He would have seen you in this very courtroom."

"When?"

"Two years ago."

"The occasion?"

"When you were tried for offences comprising seven instances of fraud. You were found guilty and sentenced to transportation."

A cry came up from among the attorneys. Mister Gracechurch had woke out of his sleep of disgrace. He remembered: oh, yes—Solomon Trumpet—seven frauds—ingenious—well, well remembered!

Then five or six others—attorneys, clerks—sprang to their feet. *They* remembered! Now they remembered. Solomon Trumpet, the great fraud—tried before Lord Sheringham. Who could forget it? Who indeed? Only the man who had never been there: the man on the Bench: the false Judge!

For a moment, I saw him try to impose himself by rage: I saw the guards quietly leave the dock and make toward the Bench. I saw the clerk draw away from his suddenly ruined master—and ushers bar all possible escapes. I saw that evil man stare violently round, as if to leap out of the world. Vainly, I tried to catch his eye—but his looks were too far flung.

Then he seemed to vanish, as if he had indeed leaped out of the world like some strange monster with his great robes flapping. For my next sight of the Bench found it empty of all save his posy of rue. The guards must have seized him and taken him away. It was over, and we had won.

173

Chapter Twenty-five

THERE was pandemonium! For twenty minutes it was impossible to be heard. Old gentlemen jumped up and down to see over their neighbours! Screams and shouts as they landed on feet not their own. Then—"For he's a jolly good fellow!", riding the storm of noise.

Who's a jolly good fellow? Why! Mister Trumpet! Lord Sheringham! Jack Holborn! Tom Furnish! Mister Gracechurch—and some dozens of others who'd somehow slipped themselves into the general rejoicing.

Also several wooden posts were cracked: and, long since, Lord Sheringham received a bill for the same: *To the repair of railings in Courtroom, damaged on the Occasion of Yr. Ldship's Triumph: Two pound ten.*

His Lordship's triumph. Indeed it was. And, all things considered, he took it wonderfully well.

In the courtroom he had, plainly, great difficulty in restraining his tears of joy that all had turned out so well. And this effort gave him a kind of grandness that was deeply affecting. Once inside the coach—the rich-smelling Sheringham coach that was to carry us to Dover Street—he shook hands with each of us very solemnly with:

"I thank you, Mister Solomon Trumpet: I thank you, sir. And I thank you, too, Master Jack Holborn: I thank you for everything, sir."

He called me "sir" which was, you must concede, an extraordinary honour. From such a man! Even though it was spoken low and uncertainly due to the profound emotion that oppressed him at that time.

Then he pointed out some enthusiast who was managing to keep up with us, running and waving a battered, old-fashioned hat. "That fellow—d'ye see? I know him! Yes!"

He had the coachman drop to a walk so he could lean out and ask the runner how he did: a poor looking man not long out of gaol. "How were things with him now?"

Then we drove on again and he sat back, enormously proud that a man he'd once sentenced should be glad he'd returned. It helped as much as anything to sweeten the bitterness that must always have lain at back of his triumph.

For it was very plain that the sudden silences he'd fall into— mid-sentence even—and the intent looks were brought on by thoughts of his brother. That man's strange presence seemed to cling inside the coach itself: for it wasn't above two hours since he'd sat in it, boldly venomous, going the opposite way. The very silk and leather still bore his warmth and imprint . . .

Mister Trumpet, though, took to his triumph quite differently. He became oddly serious and agreeable—not that he was often *dis*agreeable, but agreeable in the sense of agreeing readily. It was always "Yes—yes, indeed—" as if everyone was more interesting than himself: yet somehow giving the impression of a vast store of goodness and wisdom inside of him that politeness alone stopped from coming out.

Only once did I see the old, quick look with its hint of mockery come back into his eyes: and that was when we got out of the coach.

All the rosy-faced, beaming servants were crowding outside Number Seventeen and an old gentleman—nothing to do with anything—a passer-by, in fact—had somehow got caught up in it all. Bewildered and irritable, he asked about him what was what, and was told:

"Lord Sheringham's back! Lord Sheringham's come home!"

"Didn't know he'd been away!" he grunted, and got as many black looks as there were faces about him. His words had bit shrewdly, like a cold draught on an unsound tooth: and Mister Trumpet's eyes flickered then . . .

But otherwise, he was all grandness and affability, responding to his lordship's desire to make much of him with a warmth I never thought him capable of.

All in all, he was a credit to his great friend and I wondered if Mister Trumpet was not going to be asked to live in Dover Street as once I had been.

Then, at last, the host of that day's visitors began to leave, till, for a few moments, Mister Trumpet and me were left by ourselves in the great yellow and gold reception room. He was looking tired and serious, and staring into the quietening air. Nothing was said between us. A ghost was come into the room: the ghost of the man we'd defeated. He was there very strongly. Mister Trumpet woke abruptly out of his reverie and found himself staring into my face. We looked into each other's eyes somewhat sadly.

In Newgate, where he was at that time, that other one must have been thinking of us very profoundly, for the whole darkening house seemed suddenly to reek of him. Most particularly he seemed to be in the cheerful, elegant bedroom which was mine alone, so I found it hard to remain in bed with the thought of him ghostlily squatting on the escritoire, watching me with his queer, fishlike eyes.

It was always on the escritoire I thought of him, monkeying with the bone church-ship that had been put there. When I drew near, he'd dissolve with a faint chuckle, and I'd look down on the needle-scored boards and seem to see two tiny figures—one him, one me—squatting side by side, and a little promise hop from one to the other like a flea.

He never spoke, but when he wished to communicate, hopped up in the air and drew huge questions on the wall.

"WHAT IS TO BECOME OF YOU?" then, smaller, "Why no word of your secret?" and, "Nothing of your confession, eh? Are they ashamed of you?"

I sat up in bed angrily, knowing it all to be unreal and most likely due to too much wine.

Nonetheless, in the morning I examined the wall he'd wrote on pretty carefully, not wanting such unpleasant communications left for other eyes to see.

But then something happened that made me go quickly and

176

craftily upstairs to look at the wall again. Coincidence breeds ghosts as quick as maggots in cheese.

For I had a letter from him: from the man in Newgate himself. A letter: *Jack Holborn, Seventeen Dover Street*; brought by the prison ordinary.

In it was nothing but generalities. Said he'd often wondered what had become of me. Now he wondered all the more. Was deeply sorry about my secret. Understood how I felt. Nevertheless, he wished me well, and would I do him the favour— the last he'd be able to ask—of coming to see him before he was hanged. He'd a great desire to meet me again: if I could see my way clear to come to him.

"See my way clear." Those were his words. I supposed he meant if Lord Sheringham and Mister Trumpet raised no objections . . . He must have expected something like that. But if so, he was wrong. They said nothing. After all, the letter wasn't altogether a surprise. He was bound to try anything: clutch at any straw. A fool would have guessed that: that he'd strike at a weakness. He wasn't the kind of man to give in till he was dead.

So they read the letter two or three times and handed it back. Certainly, they weren't surprised by it: Mister Trumpet, particularly, seemed almost angry, as if with a clumsy swindler. He told me what I'd long dreaded. The promise was no more than a shrewd guess and a cheap lie to purchase my loyalty. Nonetheless I grew irritable with him and resolved to avoid him: and when that wasn't possible, to say no more than common politeness required.

But, as things turned out, I needn't have troubled. On the ninth of December Mister Trumpet disappeared. Sometime that morning he left the house and never came back. Mister Trumpet was gone. Our clever adviser—our shrewd fellow— dear, excellent Mister Solomon Trumpet! This was a blow I never counted on.

He left a note explaining. It was in consequence of his testimony. A warrant was out against him for breaking the terms of his transportation. Mister Gracechurch—that over zealous attorney—had done it. Mister Gracechurch: I'd not forget him for that law-abiding act.

For a long time I couldn't believe he wasn't coming back. Footsteps down the street, doors opening and shutting—all made my heart leap. Then at last I came to accept it and, of a consequence, felt cold and lonely.

I wondered that Lord Sheringham didn't send after him: (something could have been done about the warrant): but he said Mister Trumpet wouldn't thank us for that. He wasn't a child, waiting to be persuaded. He was a grown man who knew full well what he was about. He'd come back of his own accord when he wanted: not before.

On December ten I got a second letter from the man in Newgate. This was a farewell, simple and quiet. He understood I would not come to him. He respected whatever reason I might have had. He did not desire to know it. He was sorry that last goodbyes should have to be so: indeed, that they should have to be at all. It seemed he'd somehow got a good opinion of me. I'd made some kind of impression on him. He thought of me often, and would continue to do so as long as he was able—which, alas, was not as long as he'd have liked. But all things good and bad must have an end: and, being something of a gentleman, he would not leave anything— least of all the world—without making proper adieus.

He ended with a charitable postscript, begging me to reward the needy lady who brought the letter. Would I give her a sovereign as, foolishly, he'd left his purse behind? He appended her name so that she might understand she was being honourably paid for a task well done. He had no wish for her to be humiliated. She was called "Mrs London".

The letter came at ten o'clock in the morning: by seven o'clock that evening, I was on my way to Newgate. This was my own decision. No-one had nudged my thoughts one way or the other. My last remaining friend, his lordship, had kept silent. With indifference, it seemed to me, he watched me drifting with the tide of my unlucky dreams. He knew I was haunted by the spectre of Mrs. London: "London" of which "Holborn" is a small part: that I wondered whether this was a last great joke being played on me. Her depressed and ravaged face was always before me—as had been intended. That she'd once abandoned a child wasn't hard to believe: but that that child might have been me was a harsh thought.

At about quarter to seven, my friend said abruptly he'd ordered the carriage for me: if I wanted to use it. Then he left the room and went into his study where a great pile of business awaited him. I put down his indifference and preoccupation to this and to thoughts of Mister Trumpet. I was sorry my problem had come at so awkward a time.

Thomas, the sturdiest of footmen, went with me in the coach: a great pudding of a fellow who kept staring at his hands all the way as if wondering what they'd do next . . .

Newgate stank like it was the bilge of all London. From half a mile off it could be whiffed. I followed Thomas: he knew the way well. He inquired of the keeper where our man might be found.

The place he was lodged in was very crowded: he liked it so. Better quarters had been offered—indeed, paid for—but had been declined. I peered through the grill.

"Will you go in?"

"In a minute—in a minute!"

The keeper and Thomas muttered and retired a little way down the passage while I continued to stare into the stewpot of a room.

He was occupied. At such a time, occupation's good for a man. Brooding corrupts and makes mad—leading to unseemly scenes at the Tree.

He had managed to keep himself neat and gentlemanly. Nothing of despair was showing. He stood out, being brisk, confident and at his ease. Others leaned, slouched, mumbled and complained to their visitors: quarrelled wearily, tried to doze. *He* remained alive. Depression excited him, making him almost triumphant as he stood above it.

A man due to be hanged in the morning drew him powerfully. Several times he went back and stared at him with the utmost good humour. The fellow was plainly frightened—white as a sheet. The thought of what was to come was sending him out of his mind. There was no cheering him up—not even with the prophecy that, pale as he now was, he'd soon turn scarlet and purple in the morning. Had he holes in his stockings? Best make sure: for he'd kick off his shoes when he danced in the air—and reveal all.

These, and several other pleasantries aggravated the unlucky man's condition till he was reduced to a jelly from which nothing, not even the pleading of his wife, could rouse him. What was left of him, lying in his chains and beating his fists on the stones and shouting incomprehensibly, was so little of a man that it was scarce worth his lady's while to continue with him. She'd best go home and consider the quicker her husband was nubbed, the better for all concerned.

But she declined to leave and did her best to comfort and get some last words of peace and affection from him, the better to remember him by.

Between whiles, she abused his tormentor at the top of her voice, saying that she hoped and prayed they'd hang him slow: that if it was her last act, she'd be there to see it—even if she'd to pawn her clothes for a pew!

Then she wondered how his fine, bold airs would survive at the Tree; and whether his horrible fish's eyes would drown in honest terror.

To all of which he laughed delightedly, praising the lady's spirit. Did she come from London? He thought as much. He liked a London lass above all others!

Then, in more serious vein—not seeming to notice the fairish crowd that had gathered round—he said:

"Madam: they'll not hang me. A gypsy foretold it at my birth. 'This one,' said she, 'will never be nubbed'." He spoke with great animation and took out his watch. "Even now my salvation should be on its way."

"Rot you," said the lady. "But I hope not."

The keeper came up and touched me on the elbow. "Will you go in now? He's expecting you."

"What do you mean?"

"He said a lad would be coming to see him at about eight o'clock. He said to bring you to him at once. Much depended on it. He was very particular."

I looked back. He was still studying his watch, indifferent to the commotion he'd set up. The time was eight o'clock, and his salvation was at hand.

To be exact, his salvation had come early and had been watching him through the grille: and now stood back, scarlet with shame. I'd not read any such hopes in his letter. I wondered if his brother had. I feared so. I'd made a miscalculation. I'd muddled the little matter of whose death would make my secret not worth the keeping. It would have had to be mine. And, until that time I'd be "Salvation Jack", always ready and willing to try for another little nibble at the carrot.

He turned away from the pair whose last night he'd ruined. An ungentlemanly act, that: the mean stealing of a few hours . . . He'd dropped in my esteem. Swagger he might—he'd fallen pretty low.

I thought of his letter with its gentle dignity and quiet regret: its calmness and resignation. I thought of his friendliness and charm—his ease of manner—. All this added up to some sort of a man: a fellow of considerable, if perverse, dignity. A great shame if it should be soured.

A strange idea struck me. I began to laugh. The idea had its comic side: or at least, a kind of comedy . . . How would it be if—if I saved him indeed? And from a far worse enemy than the gallows; from—himself?

To let him go out of the world with dignity. A rare privilege. He'd thank me for it. (Much he'd thank me!) That letter: an elegant farewell if ever there was one. Why spoil it with a vulgar: "Hullo, Jack!"? No: take temptation away. *He'd* make a better showing than the man on the floor! Only give him the chance and the world would see how a man like him met his death. Even the raging lady would applaud it!

—And God forbid that ever he should escape it!—

"Are you going in yet?"

I shook my head.

"But he's expecting you!"

"Tell him—goodbye from me: for I, too, am something of a gentleman."

All the way back to Dover Street, Thomas kept staring at me as if I was mad. I kept laughing and weeping by turns. The great joke I'd just played seemed suddenly as much on myself as on the man on whom I'd finally turned my back.

Chapter Twenty-six

HE was tried on December eighteen and sentenced to be hanged at Tyburn five days after. A Christmas gift for the Devil. I got no more letters or messages from him: he had abandoned me. Whom he pinned his hopes on in his last days, no-one knew: but there was someone; no doubt of that. He would never have given up; and, as it turned out, he never did give up. I suppose that's what gave him the appearance of dignity and courage: nothing within him but the conviction that what was going to happen, *could* not happen to him: could not because of this—and that . . .

It was generally believed—and taken for granted, even—that before the twenty-third Lord Sheringham would go into the country and remain there till after Christmas. Lord Mounteagle himself said: "You'll be going into the country, of course."

To which Lord Sheringham replied curtly: "No: I shall remain in Town. If it was me to be hanged, sir, I assure you that man would be at Tyburn to see it. He'll not drive me from my home again."

"Of course—of course—" Then Lord Mounteagle, that tremendous old man, stumped out almost humbly.

Towards the end, Lord Sheringham became obsessed with the idea there'd be an escape: and I knew for a fact he had information brought him from the prison early each morning that the night had passed without event.

Sometimes I thought he was secretly longing for something of the kind: for he'd fall into a horrified despair each time he got the news: "He's still there: still there."

He slept abominably. Night after night I could hear him pacing about: sometimes, even, he walked the streets at two and three o'clock in the morning . . . (These were days and nights when I missed Mister Trumpet most bitterly. He would have known what to say or do: which I did not.)

On the night of the twenty-second, he did not go to bed at all. I think he went out for a while and then came back to sit in the library, reading aloud to himself. At first, I thought he was muttering over the Bible: but then, I discovered to my astonishment, he was reading *Robinson Crusoe*. I never found out why, at such a time, he should turn to such a book. When I came down in the morning, it was still open beside him: and at once he began discussing it with great animation—as if he'd just come upon it.

It was raining—a fine, depressing rain that soaked without first seeming to wet. "How horrible to be hanged in the rain," I kept thinking as he rambled on. For ramble he did, passing from one thing to another disjointedly: not caring whether questions were answered or not: just so long as he could occupy the air with words instead of thoughts.

At about nine o'clock he went over to the window and would not leave it. Opposite, on the other side of the street, stood a neatly dressed fellow in black. This was the man who came from Newgate every morning: today he wore his best clothes. Lord Sheringham could not keep his eyes off him.

At half-past nine this same black-clad fellow suddenly straightened himself up from the railings. He looked intently up the street—then nodded. After which, he took off his hat and walked, bareheaded in the rain, down towards Piccadilly. He must have been soaked to the skin. It was over. Signals had been passed from the nearest point to Tyburn—across rooftops—down to Dover Street.

Then at once, absolutely at once! my friend turned round, his usually reticent face quite transfigured with a most extraordinary excitement. If there'd been any other expression—such as grief, or anguish—only the window saw it: and only for the fraction of a second. He seemed to turn so quick: and his new face lit up the room. I never saw a man with such a powerful feeling bursting out of him.

"Jack! D'ye know what day it is?"

I couldn't think. I didn't know what was expected of me.

"The day before Christmas Eve! One more day! Come on, lad! What are we thinking of in this dull room! Come out and in the Town and I'll buy ye a Christmas present! One present? I'll buy ye a dozen!"

Then, still in the same feverish excitement, he dragged me out—not waiting for the carriage, not minding the rain—out and down to the shops round Haymarket.

This was an astonishing impulse of his—entirely on the spur of the moment. For when we got to the shops he found he'd come with no money!

But the shopkeepers recognized him and were honoured to give him credit. One after another we went to. If he'd had to pay as he went, I'd not have got half as much.

I got a French enamelled watch, a pair of filigree silver buckles, a gold-topped cane, silk and velvet for a new suit, a pair of chased pistols, duelling swords—and Heaven knows what else besides: more than enough to load up a chair and send it home ahead of us!

"A Merry Christmas, Jack! A Merry Christmas!"

One thing, though, almost spoiled it: a curiously sombre thing to happen. We bumped into the black-clad fellow who'd passed the signal. He looked at us as if we were mad. But Lord Sheringham affected not to see him and plunged directly into another shop.

I had a sudden morbid desire to go after the fellow and ask him all he knew—what had happened—had it been dignified or otherwise . . . But it wasn't till many days after that I heard: and then from no certain source.

I heard he'd conducted himself very easily and confidently in the cart: that he'd accepted the ordinary's ministrations with nods and smiles—all of which made a good impression. Yet it was remarked on he never uttered a word.

It's said he was smiling even when he swung off the cart, making no effort to free himself—as so many do. It's said the only thing that alarmed him—though he must have been past it by then—was when an entirely unsuspected friend ran forward to leap at his knees and give him that last, merciful tug.

It's said that then he looked starkly horrified. But it was only for an instant as his neck was broke at once. I often wondered who that friend was. At first, I dreaded it might have been Mister Trumpet. But no-one knew him. All they could say was that it was a brisk-looking little fellow of a mildewy appearance—as if his clothes had always been left to dry on his person.

And it turned out afterward that this same friend had not done the right thing at all. For someone—the hangman most likely—had previously slipped him the silver tube to go down his throat as a preventative against death by strangulation. So he'd never have died at all but for that over-eager friend . . . Still, he'd gone with dignity. Something like a gentleman, after all.

N

I know now, of course, it couldn't have been Mister Trumpet at Tyburn. He wasn't even in London at the time. He was waiting at the Black Lion Inn at Patcham, having written to tell us so the day before. When we got back to Dover Street, pacing the chairful of presents, that letter was awaiting us.

I didn't recognize the hand: but Lord Sheringham did, and the effect on him was most marked.

He was immensely fond of Mister Trumpet: and not only for the good that gentleman had done him. He liked and admired Mister Trumpet with his whole heart: and to hear from him again—with the added pleasure of a promise to see him soon—was a very great joy indeed.

"What d'ye think, Jack? A letter from Mister Trumpet! I told ye—when he was ready, eh? And now—a letter! He writes a good hand—neat, to the point . . . We'll be seeing him soon. Is not that good news, eh? It couldn't have come at a better time! He's at Patcham. That's in Sussex—a bare fifty mile! The Black Lion . . . I know it well . . . He writes for us to meet him there . . . as soon as we can. That'll be something of a Christmas! Mister Trumpet! To think of it!

"He says—what's this? . . . the writing's cramped . . . He says he makes no promises but he may have news for ye, Jack! That's something, too, eh?

"Now—now! The time, lad! Yer new watch! The time! If we leave, say, in an hour, we could stay the night at Horley and be in Patcham by mid-morning. Christmas Eve and with Mister Trumpet! Ha! Mister Solomon Trumpet himself!"

It happened we nearly spent more than one night at Horley: for the rain turned very quickly to snow, making the road very treacherous. Then, during the night, the weather turned bitingly cold, so by morning the snow had settled everywhere, making the road indistinguishable from the general country-side. But we weren't delayed above two hours and, as we travelled, had the pleasant sensation of being first in a new land. We left tracks behind us, but before us there was none.

Then the snow gave over and the sun came out as we pulled quietly into Patcham a few minutes after noon: the snow muffling our approach and making it seem somewhat secret. We took him by surprise.

"I never expected you before tonight!" he cried. "You must have set out directly you got my letter!"

"Within the hour—within the hour!"

He was livelier than I'd ever known him and was bursting to confide. But politeness constrained him to hear all we had to tell him first. He bore it amiably, and we obliged by making it brief.

The events we had to tell of were cheerless enough, and out of keeping with the agreeable parlour and lively fire round which we sat. So we finished and drank each other's health in hot punch: after which we sat down to a luncheon of excellent pork pie.

"Well," said Lord Sheringham. "Your news. This lad here has been bubbling with excitement since yesterday!"

Good Mister Trumpet laughed and waved his fork. "Will you not wait for the savouries? Or at least for the sweet?"

"No. We'll not wait another instant. If you keep us in suspense any longer, Jack and I will leave directly!"

So, somewhat ruefully, Mister Trumpet capitulated with the following: "My news is that Jack, here, is no orphan!"

"What? What? Impossible! I don't believe it!"

"It's true. I swear it."

"But this is amazing! This is astonishing—this is remarkable . . . wonderful—wonderful! A most fantastic thing! What d'ye think, Jack? Mister Trumpet here has found yer mother! I don't know what to say to ye, Trumpet—ye've done a marvellous thing! Eh, Jack?"

But I could find no words to say to my two friends at that time. I don't believe they expected any. Instead, I showed my gratitude by finishing my pork pie as rapidly as I was able. Then, when I was enough in command over my spirits, I asked him where she was. He answered she was barely two miles distant. He had been out visiting about the house that very morning.

I asked him if he'd seen her. He said no: he'd fully intended to leave that privilege first to me. Then Lord Sheringham asked him how it had been done: how, with so little to go upon, he'd achieved so notable a success?

To which he made as full and intelligible a reply as he was able, interrupted at every turn by question and counter-question, demands for more detail, requests for less, until he was reduced to the situation of almost apologising for the way he was telling of his own ingenious achievement.

By the time he'd got to the plum-pudding, he gave up and would not go on till he'd received an absolute assurance, from each of us in turn, that there'd be no more interruptions. After all, was it so much to ask that he should have the pleasure of telling the tale when I should so soon have the joy of reaping its reward? We gave him our assurances and he was able to finish.

"So I advertised."

He waited for this to take effect. "I advertised in the neighbourhood of St Bride's."

"As simple as that?"

"It would have seemed less simple if I hadn't explained! I advertised in elegant and select terms, nicely calculated to stir sentiment rather than greed. I advertised that the male child (that's you, Jack, old son!) deposited in the Church's keeping one June evening fourteen years ago, was still surviving and in easy circumstances but missing his mother sorely. If she—or any who knew of her—would call upon S. Trumpet Esq. much would be learned to mutual advantage."

"And she came?"

"Close upon forty came. That June must have been a mighty crowded month in St Bride's porch! Now, of that anxious forty, maybe twenty-five read only that part of my advertisement that related to 'easy circumstances'. Even to S. Trumpet, that was plain. Of the others, maybe fourteen read only that part that related to 'missing his mother sorely'. Had nothing else offered, I might have settled on one of them: one or two among them being fine ladies who'd do no-one a disservice by becoming his mother."

"But—?"

"But something else did offer. The fortieth. One came who'd read and digested the entire advertisement: so much so that she put me right in a mistake I'd made. *July*, she said: a young widow of her acquaintance had been forced, by poverty and despair, to do such a sad thing in the *July* of that year. Was I sure it was June? For she was sure it was July.

"Where was this widow now? I asked, expecting to be told she was dead. But nothing of the kind! The good lady furnished me with all I needed to know: and since then, I've made certain she spoke the truth.

"So, Jack, old fellow, your secret now lies with me. Will you promise to save me thrice in exchange for it?"

"Trumpet!"

"Mister Trumpet," said I gravely, leaving my pudding and rising to my feet as the occasion seemed to demand, "Mister Trumpet, I'd promise that gladly whether you had my secret or not."

"Thank you, old son. Now I feel repaid. She lives in a manor house, two miles south of here: the village of Preston. Her name is—you must prepare yourself for a great surprise here, something truly astonishing—the most astonishing thing of all, I'd say—her name is Mrs Holborn!

"So d'you see, Jack, right from the beginning you've been yourself without knowing it!"

I sat down. I thanked him. I thanked Lord Sheringham: then I thanked Mister Trumpet again. Then we all three drank more healths in hot punch and I renewed my offer of saving Mister Trumpet's life whenever he cared to endanger it in my presence. As many times as he chose, I assured him.

When I'd done, he told me what little more he knew of the mysterious lady. Her husband, my father, had been killed in the wars before I was born and left her, most desperately young with a burden that drove her near out of her mind. So that was why, shortly after my birth, she'd commended me to God as embodied in the porch of St Bride's.

He warned me not to expect too much. She was not in easy circumstances. She lived in the Manor House as the house-keeper: no more than that. The Baronet and his Lady who owned the property were understood to be a very proud couple with a reputation for not keeping a servant above a month if he or she turned out to be less than perfect. Mrs Holborn had been in their employ for close on fourteen years. From which Mister Trumpet had formed an agreeable opinion.

Now followed an animated discussion on the propriety of calling at the Manor House that very afternoon. This was hotly canvassed against by Mister Trumpet, who had grown very nice in his courtesies. Send in our compliments, by all means— and beg leave to attend tomorrow, which, being Christmas Day, would be more sure to find Sir Bertram and Lady Hodge in an amiable state of mind. There was no sense in antagonising them by seeming incivility. After all, though Lord Sheringham might have his good name to recommend him, Mister Trumpet and Master Holborn had nothing but their good manners.

But Lord Sheringham and me won the day and Mister Trumpet was forced to give in, though not without com-plaining it was against his better judgement. It was then agreed we should leave directly we had made ourselves presentable so all might appear in the most elegant light possible on this truly wonderful occasion.

In the coach, it was only natural my thoughts should turn entirely on what the immediate future was to bring. I must admit that I'd felt a bit dashed to learn that I was always to be Jack Holborn: but then I came to accept it and felt almost glad I wouldn't be required to change a name I'd got so used to.

That my mother was only a housekeeper, troubled me surprisingly little—considering how high my hopes had sometimes flown. I put this down to the fear I'd once had of being too closely related to a certain Mrs London.

The only thing, in fact, that made me less than entirely joyful, was that I was not coming to her in the grand style I'd always hoped. True, I had my fine friends to lend me lustre: but, them apart, nothing with me of material happiness.

I considered we would probably settle somewhere in fairly modest circumstances, brightened by visits to and from a pair of rich and splendid men. This gave me some comfort, and I fell to hoping my mother would take to Lord Sheringham and Mister Trumpet as whole-heartedly as I had done: and that they, in turn, would dote on her. My own feelings in that last direction, I never dared approach.

"It should have been Christmas Day," said Mister Trumpet bitterly, when we were approaching the House itself.

"Why, man, why? What difference now?"

"Because I have a present for him. It should have waited. It would have been more appropriate."

"Then give it him tomorrow."

"No: I promised it should be given when it would signify most. And that, I fancy, is now . . . Here, Jack, a Christmas present—a day too soon—but a Christmas present nonetheless—from . . . from you know whom. Take it and be happy."

Somewhat irritably and awkwardly, he thrust something into my hands. The feel of the rough canvas was at first bewildering—and then most heartbreakingly familiar. I could not, by any manner or means, hold back a great quantity of tears. This was a very moving moment to be reminded of unlucky Mister Morris.

Mister Trumpet had just given me the dead little master's forgotten bag of jewels. Not as rich as the treasure I'd once squandered—but worth, maybe, half a million pounds!

"He said to give it when you'd got sense enough to use it well. I don't think that day is arrived—or ever will—but I'm hoping a certain lady will be more provident than her son."

"You should have—hm—waited, Trumpet!" I heard Lord Sheringham mutter. "The lad is quite beside himself with emotion. His eyes will be terribly reddened and swollen when he goes in to meet her!"

Chapter Twenty-seven

LORD SHERINGHAM presented his compliments and begged leave, together with his two friends, to wait on the Hodges. They were vastly astonished and quite bowled over by the grandness of their visitor. Lady Hodge, a thin, nervous person with a quantity of red hair held down by a cap, was wild with excitement and divided her attention between his lordship's card and the great man himself. For, after all, Lord Sheringham might soon be gone, but his card would remain for ever.

Sir Bertram, on the other hand, attended to Mister Trumpet and me: finding it more comfortable to be overbearing with a plain "Mister" and "Master". In a wonderfully short time we learned how large was his park, how numerous his servants, and how strictly they were kept in their place.

"A—ah!"

For the moment, I thought it was a rook, alarmed: but it was Lady Hodge, learning why we had called. A very genteel, mortified sort of scream marked her receipt of the news. She was gone quite livid—a very uncommon colour for one of her complexion—and was staring at me very dreadfully.

"Sir Bertram—oh, Sir Bertram! D'you know for what his lordship's come?"

"No, I do not, ma'am. I left it to you to find out. You are very good at such things! You have a nose for them!"

"We thought it might be on account of being held up by the snow, didn't we, Sir Bertram," said she, disregarding his rudeness.

"*You* thought that. *I* was satisfied to keep my thoughts to myself."

"Then you thought it might be on account of your great doings on the Bench. You thought his lordship might be come to congratulate you."

"No, ma'am, I did not! Though if he had come on that score, I'd not have been surprised."

"Well, Sir Bertram, whatever you thought, you couldn't have conceived of the truth. He has come" (another terrible glance at me)—"they have *all* come to—to see *our Mrs Holborn*!"

The effect on Sir Bertram was remarkable. He flew at once into a passion which Lady Hodge regarded with the utmost complacency. "What's she done? What's she done? *I* never liked her! Get her out of my house instantly!"

"I knew you would take it like that, Sir Bertram. That's your nature. What would the great Lord Sheringham be doing here after a common criminal—like he was a simple peace officer? He's come, sir, to tell her that boy yonder— what you're nourishing in your bosom—is her son!"

This piece of news would have provoked him still further—had he not been begged to remember that, no matter whose son I turned out to be, I was also his lordship's companion.

So he contented himself with eyeing me and muttering I'd best be getting along to the servants' quarters to meet with whomsoever I chose. No such meeting was to take place in his parlour. He would countenance no such odious thing.

"Would it make any difference, sir," said Mister Trumpet, mildly, "if you was to know that Master Holborn is exceedingly rich? That he has, in that canvas bag you see him clutching, sufficient wealth to purchase your Park, House *and* servants—and never feel the pinch?"

"It would indeed," replied Sir Bertram honestly. "It would indeed."

And thereafter, he regarded me in so amiable a light that I came almost to like him: and he suffered Lady Hodge to send for Mrs Holborn without another word of protest.

"This is not well done," muttered Mister Trumpet. "This should have been in private."

"Stuff and nonsense!" murmured his lordship. "There's nothing to be ashamed of in honest sentiment and emotion! Such scenes as this do all our hearts good!"

"You sent for me, ma'am?"

She had a truly pleasing voice: gentle without being humble. I was not looking up at the time. Many things about the room seemed suddenly to claim my attention: Sir Bertram and Lady Hodge, chiefly . . . he was reluctantly standing and regarding his lady very disagreeably: as if the whole awkward situation was to be laid at her door.

I heard Lord Sheringham mutter something in a low voice, and Mister Trumpet clear his throat . . .

"Oh my dear Mrs Holborn!" sniffed Lady Hodge. "I don't know how to tell you—"

"Is it—bad news, ma'am? Please, I beg of you, let me know at once!"

(How well, how very well she talked.)

"His lordship here—Lord Sheringham, y'know—oh Mrs Holborn—I'm afraid we shall be losing you!"

"Lady Hodge! I don't understand!"

"His lordship here will have to tell you—for I'm sure I cannot! It's so—so—He's come all the way from—I don't know where—to tell you something! Oh Mrs Holborn! We shall be losing you!"

"Ma'am . . . Mrs Holborn . . . I—we have some—um—news for you . . ."

"Yes, Lord Sheringham?"

"We—that is, he, Mister Solomon Trumpet has found—
Here, Trumpet, man! *You* finish what you began!"

"There's no need, Sheringham. I think the lady's guessed."

I was looking at Sir Bertram when the room grew odd. I
felt that someone was watching me, even staring at me. I did
not feel equal to turning round. My friends whispered "Jack!",
then made Sir Bertram sniff and smile by adding, "His name is
Jack, ma'am."

She has exceedingly clear grey eyes, capable of remarkable
warmth and humour—as indeed is everything about her: her
quick movements, her sudden smiles, her laughter and her
elegant country dancing, which she manages with a most
wonderful mixture of comedy and grace.

In short, she is so much better than I ever could have imagined. There is nothing mawkish or sentimental about her.
Indeed, though she was weeping with pleasure when I turned
and discovered her to be kneeling beside me, her tears were
no more than my own: and together they made less of a flood
than Lady Hodge's, who was too easily moved by far.

The effect of all this salt water was most contagious, for
Sir Bertram tried in vain to borrow a handkerchief to remove
"a speck from his eye": but all such articles were fully in use
at that moment—even Mister Trumpet's.

"Dy'ye know," exclaimed Lord Sheringham, "there's
enough brine in this room to float another *Charming Molly*!"

We stayed to dinner: we stayed that night: and the next day
being Christmas, we stayed then also and enjoyed what Sir
Bertram called a "country Christmas".

This really began with our dinner—though we were only six
at table. A further heavy fall of snow had delayed some neighbours who were to have come, so the Hodges were glad of us.

"So you see, Mrs Holborn, we shall be losing you," said
Lady Hodge yet again.

"But surely, ma'am, some arrangement could be made?
Or are you set on my going?"

"Oh no, my dear—but you've seized hold of quite the wrong end of the stick! Hasn't she, Sir Bertram?"

"Ah, Mrs Holborn, we'll be sorry to lose you—but that lad of yours—lord! he's worth a mint of money! And all in that dirty canvas bag!"

"You're joking, Sir Bertram! It's not possible!"

"I never joke about money, Mrs Holborn. Ask the lad himself."

"Jack," said she, her hand on mine, "what have you in that bag?"

"Half a million pound, ma'am—give or take a shilling—in diamonds, rubies, emeralds and other oddments."

"Jack! Be serious! What have you hid there?"

She would not believe me till I showed her—there, at once, at table. She was astonished. She could scarcely believe her own enormous eyes. She stood up: sat down: spilled a glass of wine: apologised for it—all in a dream.

"But this is too wonderful! Where does it come from? Oh! Jack, where did you get it? Whose was—is it? Jack! You must give it back!"

"But it's mine! Ours—yours!"

"That's true, Mrs Holborn," put in Mister Trumpet. "It belongs to Jack: every penny of it!"

"That's so, ma'am," agreed Lord Sheringham. "It was a gift—a bequest, rather, from a—a strange little man now dead. I promise you, ma'am, Jack came by it honestly: and most honourably."

"Do you see now," I cried, "if Lord Sheringham himself says it, you *cannot* doubt it! We are rich—exceeding rich!"

"So you see, Mrs Holborn," said Lady Hodge, sententiously, "you cast your cakes upon the waters and now they have returned a thousand-fold.

"For he must know—he must be told, else he'll forever fear the worst of you for all your pleasant looks and elegant cooking; he must understand all you did through the long years—with Sir Bertram's and my consent.

"That you never forgot him—never! And that you wept for all of your first year with us, and begged Sir Bertram, here, to pay every penny of your wages to the Verger of St Bride's in the fond belief that that unscrupulous man would find out your child and succour him. And you yourself were to be left with nothing.

"Oh yes, madam! It must all come out! All your tears and lamentations and prayers that kept Sir Bertram and me awake so's it was only respect for religion that stopped us crying out for you to be silent! And then your two wild journeys to London—with Sir Bertram's consent—to see if the child still lived, and how.

"All must come out, madam: all, all! Why! would you give your own dear son a mother who seemed to have no love for him? Fie, Mrs Holborn! You have no understanding of such things!"

For an instant, my mother's eyes met mine—and I saw she *had* an understanding of such things: a great and proper one— and I was glad of it.

But now she demanded to know how my wealth was come by: everything! Sir Bertram and Lady Hodge, too, were agog to know: and, as a consequence, we didn't leave the table till well after midnight and into Christmas Day.

At first, I tried to persuade Mister Trumpet or Lord Sheringham to tell the story—as they were more capable. But they both disclaimed vigorously—in response, I think, to my mother's unspoken but eloquent plea to hear all from her prodigal son.

So I began: "My story must begin with when I boarded the *Charming Molly* at Bristol . . ." and until my two friends came onto my story's scene, all went pretty well. Then they began to interrupt and amplify and contradict so much that I nearly gave up.

But always Mrs Holborn came to my rescue, shushing my interrupters into a shamefaced quiet.

Sometimes, though, she interrupted herself—The affair of

Taplow alarmed her so greatly that, when I got to the main part, she begged me not to keep her in suspense but come out directly with whether I was killed or not when I fell to the deck. Everyone laughed loudly at this—she most of all when she understood what she'd said. Then she apologised humbly and promised, if I'd go on, she'd not interrupt again.

She kept her word and sat in a very gratifying silence through the rest of my narration. It went well: some parts plainly pleasing her more than others. She seemed very moved by the death of Mister Morris—and enjoyed the auction vastly.

I finished up quite quickly, not wanting to dwell on the darker aspects of more recent events—as they seemed not at all Christmas fare. Clapping and "bravo"s greeted my concluding, and opened the way for a lively general discussion.

"And is it all true?" began my mother. "He was really as wonderful as that?"

"Madam," said Lord Sheringham. "He has not told the half of it!"

"Thank God!" said Mister Trumpet, grown restless from keeping quiet so long.

"So really you both saw him for the first time on the self-same day?" went on my mother, troubled by nothing else. "Strange."

"That's so, ma'am. I saw him first the day Mister Trumpet came aboard. He had his back to me and was brooding over a barrel of salt pork. I laid my hand on his shoulder—but he never looked up. So I left before I was myself surprised."

Then Mister Trumpet took over, and then Lord Sheringham again—enlarging on this point and that till my mother flung up her hands in comical despair, crying:

"Enough! Enough! I cannot take it all in! You make me want to laugh and cry with pride—and wish I could keep all of you together for ever and ever! Oh! gentlemen! I swear I sha'n't sleep a wink tonight!"

Next day—or, to be exact, the same day after we'd slept

and come down to the front parlour, a council of war was held; it being generally agreed that six heads were superior to one. The subject of the day, viz. the Holborn estate, was debated long and earnestly. The wisdom of Lord Sheringham, the shrewdness of Mister Trumpet, the pride of Sir Bertram and the conversation of Lady Hodge, all made themselves felt: and my mother and I were condemned to listen.

It was decided that we should purchase a small Town house in the neighbourhood of Dover Street—and also rent a country estate at Lancing, which was not half a day's ride from Preston, and even closer at hand to Lord Sheringham's own estate at Shoreham.

Beyond that, the best masters should be found for me so that I might, someday, adorn any profession for which I showed the smallest aptitude. Otherwise, our time should be spent between Lord Sheringham and Mister Trumpet, with occasional visits to the Hodges.

Most of this has long since come to pass, save for the frequency of our seeing Mister Trumpet. He is so often away— and not on account of Mister Gracechurch's indictment which was happily quashed: even lawful Mister Gracechurch coming to think that some virtues should be rewarded in this world and not left entirely to the next. I think it is the White Lady that lures Mister Trumpet, particularly in the Spring when he grows most restless to be off again. But always, no matter where from, he manages to come back for Christmas.

Often, when we have other visitors, my mother asks me to re-tell some part of my adventures. But lately she complains that I've altered this or that part of them: and missed out something important altogether.

She has become a great Authority on them, and has advised me to write them down. Which at last I have done.

God save the King!

THE END